CRUSHES, CRIMES AND

Cool Jazz

A Nikki Rodriguez Mystery

M.A. HANSEN

I0677058

Prologue

The cold and windy evening made the trees cry a high pitch into the black sky. The stranger got in the car and watched... The couple drove off together, meeting at their secret rendezvous for their weekly affair. Following them was easy; they thought they were so discreet, so clever. Thought the stranger...

The stranger had followed behind them at a safe distance. Behind a large Maple tree with a good view of the couple, they exited the car and ran to the house. There they were, kissing and holding each other. It was obvious they couldn't wait to open the door; their passion and lust were disgusting. Once they were in, the stranger got out of the car, hurried across the street, past a lamp post, and crept to a window on the side of the house.

The darkness lit by candlelight reflected their shadows that speckled and danced on the walls. The heavy sounds of breath and their cries of satisfaction were now hysterical with pleasure.
The stranger watched them, knowing that they needed to be stopped! How dare that little evil harlot ruin everything?

This affair would not get in the way of the plans the dark stranger had. The stranger felt a twisting and unsettling mulch in the pit of their stomach. A sickness that needed to be extinguished!

The harlot would be leaving, oh yes, she would be leaving very soon, that was certain! And then everything would be back to normal, oh yes, back on track. The future would continue as it had been planned. All will be right again. The stranger thought. Soon, very soon, she will be gone.

CHAPTER 1

Welcome to Rancho Niguel

I was winding up a little tune from Ella Fitzgerald, a 1940s icon of jazz and one hell of a singer. One that set the stage for so many sultry voices in jazz that came after her, I am one of those singers. So here I was singing my heart out, "It don't mean a thing if it ain't got that swing doo-wop, doo-wop, Doo-wop." Jamming in a one-car garage in my new condo complex. One with a custom-fitted acoustic ceiling and acoustic side panels for great sound and balance. It was around five o'clock, this evening being Tuesday as well as Thursday nights. The usual practice times for five of us, beautiful and intelligent girls from school, who got together and formed our band, Little Black Dress. We have been together for five years, and well, we don't have any record deals yet, but we do ok. Practice usually ends at 6:30 pm, and I couldn't wait to head over to the mall across the street to have a bite to eat. Boy, was I starved. No lunch today. No, I'm not dieting, for me, it's a

forbidden word; I just enjoy food too much. By now, my headache was beginning to take form, and believe me, I could do without a migraine. We finished off the song, made some notes to change the last bar of the piece, and called it a night.

I pushed the button on the wall to open the garage door, and slowly, the white door rolled up to a beautiful sight. The San Bernardino Mountains high above the city of Rancho Niguel, California. The June sunset had changed the Robbin's egg blue sky to a burnt orange with strips of purple running through it. The golden palm trees swayed slowly in the California breeze. It was lovely. Although I am biased, born and raised a Southern California girl from Rancho Niguel, I grew to appreciate the small contributions the smog made here in the valley. It translated into some of the most beautiful sunsets imaginable. I know, right, harmful gases lend a hand to beautiful sunsets. Strange, to say the least.

I closed the garage, and again, it slowly rolled down to a thud. Our equipment is stored here, too, because my place is the only one big enough for all the instruments, sound equipment, costumes, and mics and sound boxes, the whole enchilada. I can't park my car in there, and that is a con, but at least I have an open parking spot in front of my condo, and we are allowed two reserved spaces, which isn't bad.

The band gets steady work, we play for local ceremonies, weddings, grand openings, and city swarays. Our biggest gig is Wednesday and Friday Night at Kendle's Kannery Restaurant.

Our sultry jazz tunes have made us a popular dinner band for the last two years or so. For the other girls, this is a part-time gig, but for me, it's been my full-time job since I invested in a computer company that had success, and now I'm able to live off my return from that investment. It's not a lot, but it's enough to cover all of my expenses, and the moola I make from the band is a little extra frosting. The girls went to their cars, parked off the street beside the complex,

6

and headed off. Only my best friend, Roxy, the drummer in the band, hung around with me. We were on our way to go and grab a quick bite at the outdoor mall across the street. You'll know that just about every city has an outdoor mall in California, just one of those perks we're very lucky to have.

"Can you smell the garlic bread?" Roxy said as she sniffed the air with great delight. Her bleached blond hair was put up in a tight bun today with Chinese chopsticks sticking out. Tight black capris and a black halter top completed her look. Mirror in hand and sliding a glossy red lipstick over her full lips, smacking them to perfection, she said, "I'm starving, I want lasagna."

"That sounds good," I said, indulging in the idea of oozy mozzarella with vine-ripened tomatoes and fresh basil baked over a ricotta-filled, luscious lasagna!!! But mid-way through my thought, I sensed something wasn't right... "It also smells like," Well, I was going to praise the beautiful smells coming from the restaurants, but instead, it smelled like something was terribly wrong.

"It smells like something is burning!" I responded.

We walked around the garage to see the condo complex; the three-level building painted a calm sage green loomed before us.

The sight that we were dropping our jaws for was the big blazing fire that smoldered with orange flames of rage.

"Oh my God, Nikki, your condo complex is going to go up in flames," Roxy said. Breaking me, Nicole Rodriguez, from the shock that was displayed on my 28-year-old face.

In the distance, the screeching sound of sirens came from Rancho Nigel's finest fire department, running at lightning speed to fight this fire.

My first thought was, whose condo was sitting in flames? Was it my friends, the newlywed couple, the Zanes, Kiana and Craig? The white and blue fire trucks, two of them to be exact, came rolling in through the front entrance to the complex. Roxy and I gathered around a small crowd of my neighbors who were running out of their homes. Some I knew, some I didn't.

Mrs. Green ran toward me; she was still in her light blue scrubs with SpongeBob dancing on them. As head nurse at Rancho General in the pediatric ward, she often pulled in 10-15-hour day shifts. She had a very likable Sally Field look to her that was comforting, plus her favorite word was "tootles." Just like Sally Field in the 1960s TV show Gidget.

"Oh, Nikki, I can't believe this! A fire in our beautiful new complex, I just bought this condo with my ex-husband's life insurance policy, I can't be homeless!" She was tearing up now, and I hugged her to comfort her. "It will be okay, I promise they'll put out the fire right away."

Mrs. Green, a recent widow from her second husband of five years, died from a heart attack on their vacation to the Grand Canyon. Tell me how much that sucks.

Her job and her new home were all she had left. I know she works a lot to fend off loneliness. Mrs. Green often told me it wasn't getting any easier at 61 years old in the dating world for the baby boomers.

"Nikki!" I heard my name again and turned. Martin and Oliver Dunner were jogging along the path from the garden that surrounded the enormous pool.

Sweaty and red-faced, the couple in their matching black sweat suits stopped and stared in horror. Catching his breath and gulping down a bottle of Fiji water, Martin asked. "Nikki, what happened?"

Mrs. Green spoke first, "Oh, Martin dear, it's just horrible, our home is going up!" She grabbed a Kleenex from her pocket and dried her eyes. "I don't know, guys, we just finished band practice," Roxy replied. Martin looked worried but kept his cool, his handsome face and short dark hair cut a sleek look of a G.Q. model.

"Nikki, go find out what's going on and whose condo is burning," Roxy said as she comforted Mrs. Green.

Oliver stopped drinking his bottle of water, wiped his brow with a pressed white handkerchief, and said, " C'mon, Nikki, you've got the fireman connections, see if he knows anything." A look of absolute fear in his watery blue eyes, he ran a hand through his highlighted blond hair in frustration. Then the color drained from his tanned face, and he looked closely above at the orange blaze coming from the windows in the condo.

"I think that's Chanel's place!"
Now, many people had gathered, the fire department had evacuated the entire building, and even people from across the street from the mall had formed a circle of spectators. I even saw NBC 4 with their helicopter circling the scene.

9

There were some police holding back the crowd with wooden barriers, keeping them at a safe distance. I left my friends and snuck around the barrier when an officer directed a group of reporters back behind the line of safety. Sneaky that I was, I hid behind the side of one of the fire trucks and blended in with all the first responders. "Nikki, what are you doing here?" Lieutenant Buchman said as he stood there in his coat and boots. "I live in this building, on the second floor. Has anyone been hurt?" he put his hand on my shoulder in a fatherly way and said,

"You're not supposed to be in this area; it's dangerous." He said with concern. My stubbornness left me standing in front of him. My arms crossed over my chest, and my red Converse shoe tapped the sidewalk for him to respond.

He sighed, shook his head and gave in. "Well, I'm not supposed to say anything yet, but we found a body, a woman, but we don't have an ID on her yet, that's all I can tell you." My look of confidence faded after hearing that someone didn't make it.

Now I was feeling pretty bad for someone who was gone. "Oh my God, that's terrible." My face was in complete shock at what the Lieutenant had told me.
The flames had disappeared, and all that was left was fading black smoke that escaped into the deep purple sky.
"Thanks," I said. Lieutenant Buchman was a father of two 20-something twin girls, and a forlorn look on his weathered face showed his grave sadness for the loss of the young woman.
We were interrupted by a good-looking detective in a dark suit and a

pair of Oakley sunglasses. "Lieutenant Buchman, I'm Detective Paul Anderson." he extended his hand, and the two shook.

"Can I have a moment of your time?"

"Sure, detective, excuse me, Nikki."

I waved bye to Lt. Buchman.

I saw the coroners pull up in their black GMC Yukon; they took out their gear and walked past the yellow tape that had been put up. The CSIs made their way to the fire truck and passed me into the courtyard of the condo. Each building of condos came with its own courtyard with lush gardens, along with teak wood benches. Each front door faces the courtyard, and each balcony has a view of the mountains or the mall. The quaint park atmosphere is what I liked best about this place.

The team of firefighters came out of the condo, their voices fully audible as they walked out from the courtyard. "Hey, Nikki." A few men said as they took off their yellow jackets and wiped their foreheads. "Hi Tank, Hi Brinks," I said. "If you're looking for Matt, he's coming out, don't worry," Brinks said, then he looked back to see if anyone else besides Tank was listening. "I have to tell you, your boy was worried. When we got the call to this location, he flew out of the house; he kept calling you, BUT NO ANSWER!" They both repeated in unison. Tank and Brinks were the two "old guys," as they were referred to, the best and the most respected in the city. Marine Corps War vets from Riverside, CA. Still strong and handsome, with respect from all of the men in their house. They graduated from the fire academy some years after the war, and they have been best friends since then; their wives are best friends, too, and they usually take vacations together and talk all the time about their grandkids. They are both going to retire soon. The band has been hired by the city to play at the retirement party this coming September, and I can't wait.

"Nikki," Matt Stevens walked out of the courtyard with his brow dripping with sweat. He yanked off his jacket and wiped his forehead with a towel that Brinks threw to him. "Thanks, buddy." He gave me an I'm so glad you're okay look.

"Take a walk with me!" he asked. I waved bye to the fire crew, and then Matt and I walked to the back of the fire truck. He pulled me close, "Thank God you're ok. I was trying to call you, but you never answered my calls!" He was concerned, but then became a ranting, worried father. "We get a call about a fire at the location of your place, and then I can't get a hold of you, and then we find a woman lying on the floor dead." he was talking fast now, running through the scenario that was in his head and talking by motions with his hands. His concern for me was so sweet. What a guy. "Matt, you know I turn off the phone during practice, we were finishing up when I came out and saw the fire, besides, you know that's not my unit, I'm in B-24." I felt like saying ok, can I go to my room now. He realized his behavior and backed off; his hands dropped off my shoulders. "Over the radio, D-24 can sound like B-24 look, I was just worried about you," he said with sweet sincerity. "Even though we broke up a month ago." It came out fast, and I kicked myself secretly in the ass for saying it. Now I was being a jerk. Why did I get this way? "I know!" he said, putting a little distance between us. Matt and I had been on again and off again for quite some time; our two-year relationship was always on the rocks. I had only been living in Rancho Niguel for a short time when Little Black Dress had a gig to play at the annual Harvest festival in town. I was up on stage singing "The Way You Look Tonight" when he caught my eye. He was standing by one of the fire trucks dressed in his navy blue uniform, passing out stickers and candy to all the children who gathered around the large fire truck, asking him a million questions about being a firefighter. He was all smiles and very patient with all the kids. I liked that about him. After the song was over, he walked up to me, complimented my singing, and then asked me out on a date. We had an instant connection, just like friends who had known one another forever. Since then, we have been in a relationship that has never moved on to another level. I liked that about us; it was easy that way, with no restrictions or real commitment that I wasn't ready for. I still felt independent and free to make my own choices. Besides, we also have very busy lives, I mean, with the band playing weekends and late nights, and with Matt's schedule, he practically lives at the fire station. There's no room for anything else. I brought it down a notch and went for being nice and grateful; it's much better for me than a negative attitude.

"Matt, look, thank you for your concern, it's nice that you care about me, but." I started to say.

"Nikki, you know I care," he said pointedly.

He grazed my hand and left it there for a few minutes. Of course, he did. A month ago, he asked me to move in with him, and then I told him we should take a break from each other. I wanted to change the subject, and fast, I didn't want to talk about this again, especially not here at this time. Matt could usually read me very well, so I assumed he thought the same thing. This wasn't the place to go into our relationship flaws. So he kindly changed the subject and gave me a little distance once again. "Do you know who lives in D-24?" he asked me.

"That's where Chanel O'Conner lives." Bingo!! Oliver had been right. The coroner came out of the courtyard with a black body bag on a gurney. One of the CSIs coming out said, "Yes, we have an ID, her name is O'Conner, Chanel, she said, speaking to the waiting detective Anderson. He nodded and headed to the gurney, looked at what was left of the charred remains, and then zipped up the bag and nodded again. I could only see part of her burnt body that, to me, was unrecognizable except for what was left of the platinum blond hair, and I knew it was her. They wheeled her into the black SUV that said CORONER in white letters. I looked away in horror. I walked away with my hand to my mouth. "Are you ok?" Matt asked, following me to see if I was all right. "I'm going to be!" I said, trying not to vomit. "Here, sit down," he grabbed my hand and led me to the nearest seat. I sat on the bumper of the fire truck to catch my breath. I was pretty shaken up, that was for sure, but I brushed it off, the bile in the back of my throat and the knotting feeling building in my stomach. "I'm going to be fine," I said, taking small, deep breaths. I saw Detective Anderson head to the burned-out condo, talking to the CSI people and making some comments about smoke alarms.

"So Matt, what started the fire, and what about the smoke alarms and the sprinkler system, all the condos have them." He sat next to me on the bumper. His deep blue eyes searched for an answer to my question. "There was a tall candle holder which probably held four pillar candles, and as far as we can tell, the candles fell over, hitting the drapes, very common, and then the fire rose to the ceiling and to the walls. The smoke alarm in the living room didn't have any batteries in it, and the sprinklers were jammed. The one in the bedroom went off, but the fire started in the living room, and Chanel was lying on the floor where the fire started, so she most likely died by smoke inhalation." "Matt, these condos are new. Why would the batteries be dead after four months?" I asked. "Well, maybe the batteries were old, or some people remove the batteries and think they will replace them right away, but then never get around to it. It happens all the time, but as far as the sprinklers being jammed, I would guess that someone wanted to make sure she was dead." I went numb again. Murder! Who would murder Chanel? She was a nice person and didn't seem like the type to have a lot of enemies. Was this random, or was she the victim of someone she knew? My head began to throb with pain. "Hey, honey, are you ok? Maybe one of the medics should look at you," he said, standing up and taking hold of me. "I'm fine, Matt, just a little shock and lack of food." I had a serious case of the roller coaster stomach after all I had just seen. Add the growling stomach and hunger pangs that were coming on strong; it was a bad mix. "You should get something to eat." Was he inviting me out? He was so gracious when he spoke to me that I guess I assumed he wanted to go out and have a delicious meal with a glass of my favorite Cabernet and console away my worries. Without thinking it through, and only going for what I wanted to happen. I just blurted out! "You want to join me?" I asked, knowing he got off work in an hour. He looked a bit surprised, he smiled, and looked to consider my invitation. I knew he wanted to take me up on it; he had missed me, too. Then his look changed, and his smile faded. "No, I can't," he said, picking up his jacket and helmet. Disappointed by his rejection, my face fell, but I brightened and asked, "Oh, are you on are on a new schedule?" His jaw tightened, and he replied.

"No, I have a date." He turned and started to walk away. I must have looked jilted and angry because he chuckled and said, " We broke up, remember." Well, I guess he's moved on.

CHAPTER 2

There's a new Cop in Town

I woke up to the sounds of the morning traffic on Water Creek Avenue.
People were charging down the street, running to their jobs in the city.
Running to get their kids to school on time or running to get their
nonfat double lattes with bagels and cream cheese. I opened the
curtains to let in the sunlight and started to think about the events that
happened last night. The fire and the death of a fellow neighbor, I was
stunned! It had all happened so fast. I turned on the TV. The KTLA
morning news (the funny guys) is what I call them because of their
morning comedy and lunacy, which in LA is quite the hit. It was the
second story of the news, "local woman in Rancho Niguel, Chanel O'
Conner, the administrative assistant to the mayor of Rancho Niguel,
was found dead in her new Condo complex. Police are saying it was a
homicide."

They showed yesterday's footage of the fire, and then a beautiful
reporter with long dark hair began interviewing Detective Anderson.
"So I have here with me Detective Anderson of the Rancho Niguel
police department. Detective, how was this woman murdered?"

Anderson was cool and calm; his dark, short hair and professional suit
matched his clean-shaven face. His shades and his golden tan were an
indication that in his spare time, he took in a lot of sun, but not too
much. It was a... I use a sunblock type of tan, a natural-looking ode to

the typical Californian. I bet he's a surfer, or so I guessed. "The deceased was killed by smoke inhalation due to the massive fire that erupted."

"Detective, do we know what or who started the fire?" The reporter asked,

"I can't say more at this time, but what we need is the help of the community. If anyone saw or heard anything odd or saw anyone unfamiliar or anything suspicious, please contact the Rancho Niguel Police Department."

"Detective, can you tell us if the victim was hurt before the fire? Is this a random act? Or is it a case of the victim knowing her killer?"
"No comment!" he said with a still motionless look.

The reporter tried a few more questions, but didn't get much of a response except "no comment" from the detective. The reporter, even with her good looks, understood she wasn't going to get any more out of Anderson and wrapped up her report. "Thank you, Detective Anderson." The funny guys came back on the news. " That was live footage of the blazing fire last night, and if anyone has any information, you are encouraged to call the Rancho Niguel Police Department at 1-800-555-1212. Your help could make a difference in this investigation. In other news, locals are concerned with the toxic water levels in Santa Monica Beach." I turned off the TV and headed for the shower.

I couldn't believe it, Matt was right, it was murder! Last night, before Roxy and I went to get a bite to eat, the police interviewed a few tenants and stated that D-24 is a crime scene and no one is to be in or near there unless they live in that corridor.

The hot water that trickled down felt good on my back. Lathering up my hair with shampoo, I kept thinking about what could have happened. I was running scenarios in my head. I was feeling paranoid and searching for some answers to this horrible tragedy. Now, if the vic knew her killer, then who would have hated her enough to commit murder? Did Chanel have an old boyfriend, or did she know something that the mayor was doing that she shouldn't have known? I had so many questions: what if it were someone here in this building? There are gardeners and pool cleaners and people delivering packages, water, and all sorts of other things. Was it a pro hit, or someone who was a career criminal who had an axe to grind with Chanel? The thought was chilling. I washed off my hair and body wash, my mind pacing and turning over ideas in my head, but I put it away for now and turned off the shower.

Starbucks was crowded today; people were gossiping about the big fire.

"Good morning, Nikki, your usual."

"Morning, Jessica, yeah, and could you throw in an everything bagel and two cream cheeses?" Oh, that glorious bagel topped with sesame seeds, poppy seeds, dried pieces of onion, and garlic, and finally topped off with really good quality cheddar cheese.

"Sure," she said,

"I guess you guys are busy today, huh?" I asked, looking around the crowd of customers.

"Yeah, did you see the camera crew out there? They are going to interview the mayor at the Cultural Arts Center today; he's having a press conference at 10 am."

She handed me my Grande drip coffee.
"Did you know Chanel?" she whispered as she leaned in for some new information. "Yes! We had some of the same friends."

"Oh, you must feel awful. I'm sorry." She said, feeling bad

"We were acquaintances; I knew her for a short time."
She looked sideways to make sure the other baristas were not listening. Jessica was a talker, a gossip kind of gal, but in a good way, with loads of information on a lot of things. She is a very social person who loves to share what she knows, but in a positive way, not to pick on anyone or make fun of them.

"I heard that Chanel's ex-boyfriend was a real bad guy. My brother's girlfriend, Blanca, works at the county probation office. Well, she said that John Amos, Chanel's ex, was one of her parolees. He did time for armed robbery, but he got out early because he struck a deal with the D.A., something about having info on some drug ring," Jessica said as she handed me my bagel. "Wow, I wonder if the police think he's a suspect."

"I don't know, but he also has committed other crimes, breaking and entering, possession of cocaine, disturbing the peace, and burglary."

"Well, it does make him look like the prime suspect, but why would he want to hurt Chanel? Did they have a bad breakup, or was she seeing someone else?"

Jessica went to the coffee grinder and put a pound of coffee in it; she hit the switch and counted to ten. Then she put the coffee in a large paper basket-style filter and slipped it into the coffee maker. "I don't know, but one thing is for sure: when he gave Blanca his new address, it was to Chanel's condo."

My manicured eyebrows shot up!
"Really, how interesting," I said.
What does that mean? Chanel works for the mayor of a very wealthy city. She has a nice place to live, a cool black convertible, and expensive clothes, but she has an ex-boyfriend from the hood that she broke up with, and now he uses her address, which didn't make sense to me.
"Look, I have to get back to work; I'll see you in Yoga class Thursday morning. I'm getting a three-day weekend come Friday, and I'm going to Palm Springs with some friends for a spa weekend. I can't wait."

She said in a shrieking, playful voice.
I took my coffee and bagel and waved goodbye,
"See ya, girly."
I had been one of the first people Jessica met here in Rancho Niguel. She was from the San Fernando Valley and moved here a few years back. We met while waiting in line at the Sprouts Market when an irate customer had a fight with the cashier over sleeping with her fiancé.

21

Jessica and I had nearly missed being smacked by an extreme catfight. We ducked at the same time and ran for the exit just as two police officers entered the store and arrested the two women. We went next door to the Italian restaurant for a drink two hours later and became fast friends. Since then, we have gone to the same yoga class and meet a few nights a month with Roxy for a girl's night out. I knew her lead on this case was reliable; I had to have her keep in contact with Blanca, and maybe more info would come.

After Starbucks, I hopped in my red bug and put the top down; the sun was shining high early on this June morning, and already it was a balmy 72 degrees. I headed down to the Culture Arts Center to catch the press conference. This new building was an addition to the new Rancho Gardens Mall that sat in front of it.

The mall, of course, carries everything I deem necessary. It consists of high-end stores Nordstrom, Macy's, White House/Black Market, Pottery Barn, William Sonoma, Crate and Barrel, Gap, Coach, Abercrombie and Fitch, Burberry, Brighton, and many fabulous restaurants. It's an all-outdoor mall, complete with park-like lawns and teak benches, cobblestone walks and water fountains, mosaics and tile murals with a vintage look, and Spanish architecture and Ironwork. The new Library was first class too, with large windows and living rooms with large fireplaces and private rooms for meetings, many computer stations, books, books, and more books. This looked like a combination of Barnes and Noble at the Ritz Charlton.

The Cultural Arts Center and the Library were housed in two separate buildings but shared the large foyer and lobby, which separated both venues.

Since I lived across the street from everything, the Mall, library, and the

Cultural Arts Center, I decided to park my bug back at the condo and walk to beat the traffic of the many news vans that were stretched along Key Ave. There were a lot of people here from the Chamber of Commerce and the city of Rancho Niguel. I spotted a few news anchors from local NBC, ABC, FOX, and KTLA; they were checking their mics and powdering their noses.

A large crowd of city committee members and the police chief had positions next to the podium where the mayor would be addressing the city, with reporters from all over.

Mayor Grant Mahoney moved to the podium, his sleek dark grey suit pressed without a wrinkle to be seen. Salt and pepper-haired, his stylish 40-something James Bond persona and sweet smile were a big hit with all the ladies. He removed a pair of black glasses and, looking handsome but distraught, he began his political speech. The reporters took their places up in front of the crowd that was gathering around the stage.

"Ladies and Gentlemen, I'd like to start by saying this is a tragedy for the city of Rancho Niguel." he looked down and took a slow, shallow breath as if the grief was too much to go on.

"I would like to say we are all sorry for the loss that has occurred. Miss O'Connor was a young and talented woman, and she will be missed in this city. Our condolences go out to her family and friends." he paused and turned in the direction of none other than Detective Anderson. "I will now turn the mic over to our head detective." There was some applause, and then Anderson took the stage.

"Thank you, Mayor Mahoney. Let me start by saying that we have some new evidence in this case. It has been discovered that Miss O'Connor was hit on the head by a sharp object, causing her to be unconscious at the time of the fire, where she perished in the flames. We do not have a suspect yet, but we are following a few solid leads and hope to have more information in the next few days."

There were reporters all calling out at the same time, all of their questions. "What object was used to kill the victim? Did she know her killer?"

Anderson was cool and calm.

"Please, ladies and gentlemen of the press, that's all we have at this time. We thank you for coming, and we ask that you stress to the public to come forward if they have any information on this case."

He had kept his black shades on the whole time, and now he excused himself from the podium and walked back to his position with the other fellow officers. Mayor Mahoney came back to the podium and finished up the press conference by saying that...

"We will have justice for Miss O'Connor; I will see to it that, as Mayor of this fine city, I will not let you down."

The sun was shining strongly now, and the press conference had ended to some cheers and a roar of applause.

It was a good thing, any longer, and everyone would be getting sunburned. Thank God for makeup with SPF. I spotted my fellow neighbors, Oliver and Martin, leaving the press conference and heading in the direction of the mall to their business, Dunner Art Gallery.

"Martin, Oliver, wait up."

They turned, and we gave hugs. Oliver looked like he hadn't gotten any sleep from the red-rimmed eyes he had.

"Hi, Nikki."

"Are you ok?" I asked.

"I 'm lacking in the sleep department; I know I just look terrible."

"You do not, "Martin blurted out.

"Oh, Martin, you're sweet," Oliver whispered while blushing.

Love! It made me miss that feeling of knowing you had someone to come home to at the end of your day. Someone to ask how your day was or if you need a back rub, or let me make you dinner. That sort of thing, the mushy, funny I'm in love, kind of stuff that everybody wants but doesn't want to admit to. I moved on from my thoughts and pressed them for their opinions on the Mayer.

"So, what did you two think of the mayor's speech?" I asked.

"Rehearsed, he was trying to keep it together, but he was going to break out in tears," Martin said. Popping a mint into his mouth.

"He's right; I mean, Mahoney was all Oscar drama there. You know, Chanel told me one time that she and Grant Mahoney were more than just working together."

Oliver told me as he checked to see if there were any other ears in the area of our conversation. I looked shocked.

"Nikki, it's true," Oliver stated

. This was new information to me; the Mayor and Chanel were an item. He is married and seems so committed to his responsibilities. It did seem shocking to me, not unusual because this sort of thing always happened in life, but just that it was a scandal so close to my circle of friends. Mentally, I began to put it together and connect the dots that I had in front of me to this murder.

"So uh they were..."

"LOVERS, and get this, he even told her he was going to leave his wife after his term in office ended and that they were going to move to some little island up in Washington state so they could get married and start a family."

"She told all of this to you two?" We had pulled out of sight from the news and the people passing by.

"Yes, she had a bad day a couple of weeks ago, and Oliver invited her over for a Margarita.

"I do make the best ones," Oliver responded.

Martin continued, "She couldn't hold her liquor, two, and she was telling us her life story and the color undies she had on. Sad, really sad girl, we felt so bad for her. She was so upset, we made her stay the night in the guest room."

"Oh, we couldn't let her go home like that poor thing." Oliver finished.

"Wow, I had no idea this was going on. After hearing all of this, let's just say that your money is on the mayor."

They both shook their head and, in unison. "No, honey, his wife!"

I was shocked again. Did the wife know all of this was going on?
I thought over this new information as we walked.
I followed Martin and Oliver back to their Art gallery in the mall to see

a new painting they had to show me. The gallery had a few people admiring paintings and browsing the sculptures on display.

"What do you think, Nikki?" Oliver asked, showing me to the back room where the new paintings came in and were stored. A large daylight basement-style warehouse in the back of the elegant gallery, racks of pottery and sculptures, and a spotless and dustless area with creative treasures from all over the world.
I took a step back to take it all in. It was awe-inspiring and simply beautiful.

"It is breathtaking." I responded
Oliver smiled. "I knew you'd love it, Nikki."

The painting was done by a newcomer named Miles. He had painted this canvas with a combination of reds, yellows, oranges, browns, ivory, black, and a subtle hint of greens. It formed an image of a red baby grand piano and a faded male piano player. A female silhouette singing at a 1950s mic, and a sax player. Along with a drummer and guitar player, all in a field of yellow roses made out of music notes, and palm trees made of thorns and green dollar bills. The sky was an orangey fire with tones of purple and deep blue. The instruments were faded too, the faces absent and yet full of life. The painting was like a dream. A fade of events that told a story that you could interpret any way you'd like. Who were they? The singer and band players, were they happy? Were they jealous or envious? Were any of them in love? Were they plotting something sinister? After all, the painting was called Killer Cool Jazz...

I headed to Sprouts Market to grab a sandwich and think hard about what Martin and Oliver had said.

Did Chanel have a future with the Mayor?

Did his wife know about it? Then what about the ex-boyfriend with a rap sheet?

How did he fit into all of this? Did he find out about Mahoney and Chanel and get enraged enough to kill her?

Or was it Mrs. Mahoney who knew and went to see Chanel to tell her to end it? There was a struggle, and then they fought, and Chanel fell, hitting her head on the coffee table in her living room, and Mrs. Mahoney, being scared, ran off, leaving poor Chanel to die in that fire. Martin and Oliver were right, Mrs. Mahoney seemed more like the right suspect; she had a motive.

My stomach grumbled as I headed to the deli counter.

"Hi, how can I help you?"

A red-haired young woman behind the counter asked.

"I'd like a Mozzarella, Roma tomato, and basil on a whole wheat roll with pesto on it."

"Coming right up."

"What, no Greek side salad to go with that?"

I turned around to see Matt holding a small green grocery basket

with two pints of vanilla frozen yogurt and a basket of strawberries and blueberries.

"No, just the sandwich. What are you doing here? Sprouts is an organic and healthy food store. I thought firemen loved ribs and lasagna and steaks and burgers." I said with a little sarcasm.

He laughed a little and shook his head.

"I'm training for a calendar again, gotta eat healthy."

"I see."

Every year, Matt was asked to pose in the yearly city Firemen's calendar that sold for the burn center at Rancho General Hospital. It was a very profitable calendar, and the money this year was going to a special camp for pediatric burn victims.

Matt's only request was to be Mr. August because that's the month of my birthday.

He enjoyed the photo shoots as well. Matt is one of the most charming guys, and people enjoyed his company.

He's fun to be around, the type of guy that's polite and helpful and will go into a burning building to save you.

"So, just dessert, no food." I asked him like a worried mom, "I came to get a turkey and lettuce on whole wheat, too. Is there anything else you'd like to know?" he smiled.

Yeah, who were you out with last night? That's what I wanted to ask.

Okay, okay, I admit I'm still hung up on Matt. I broke up with him for a stupid reason: I got scared. There, I finally admitted it. I didn't want to seem too interested in his affairs, so I played the cool card.

"No, nothing else," I said.

We had a few seconds of silence, neither of us knowing what to say.

Stay cool, I told myself. Don't let him know you are dying to know about his social life. Holding my basket, I could feel my hands grip the handle a little tighter. Trying to hold on for dear life as my imagination of his last night's whereabouts was running a marathon through my mind. I tapped my hot pink Nikes, waiting, waiting!! Good gracious, the time was going by so slowly, this was agony!! Ugg like watching an episode of The Kardashians... Ugh...

Then, without any more patience for my curiosity, I blurted out... "So, who were you with last night?"

The moment it all came from my mouth, I wanted to bite my tongue. He laughed a little; I knew he was enjoying this!

"That's none of your business anymore, remember."

The redhead girl came back out with my sandwich and said

"Here you are, ma'am, oh, hi Matt."

Big red came from behind the counter, her tight black pants and green polo shirt snug to her curvy form. She slithered to him and touched his shoulder.

"The usual for you today."

Her smile had brightened tenfold

" .Yes, Trixie, the usual." Matt replied.

"Coming right up," she flirted, walking away

. Then she turned around again and said,

"So are you free Friday night?"

I grabbed my sandwich, rolled my eyes, and walked away, fast. That had been one of the reasons why I broke up with Matt. Women like Trixie with names like Bambi and Bubbles, or the Playboy bunny type, were always coming on to him, flirting and swaying back and forth, or asking him out. The kind of girl that just had to be on his arm and feel his warm touch or his soft lips on theirs. The kind of girl who always took away someone else's boyfriend because that's the guy of the month.

He had never flirted or cheated on me; he said he wasn't like that. He said he cared for me and he would never hurt me, that he was genuine, and when he loved, it was real.

Even though I believed him, and I really did. I just ended it because I was insecure and afraid that one day, maybe he would. Maybe one day I wouldn't be enough, and every time I thought of it, it hurt. I had let him go early, rather than be left with a broken heart. Truth is, I'm still in love with him!!

CHAPTER 3

Welcome to Kendle's

This evening's gig was at Kendel's Kannery Restaurant. Kendle's was part of the many places to eat at this glamorous outdoor mall. Every Wednesday and Friday, Little Black Dress played classy dinner music to its local and visiting patrons. From 6 pm to 8 pm, we did the usual soft rock, but at 9 pm we spun out our sultry jazz tunes.

The owner of Kendle's was Kaid Kendle. He was a dot-commer from Silicon Valley, made a few million, and headed out here to open restaurants to invest in. The location here in Rancho Niguel was his first, but he opened two other locations in Palm Springs, and one is going up in Santa Barbara. He's your typical good-looking, sandy blond hair, tall, surfer type in an Armani suit that drives a silver Lamborghini. Quite a catch if you ask me, but he's not my type. Today was pretty busy in the restaurant. Usually, before 6 pm on a Wednesday, there is never a wait to sit down.

But today it seemed like NASCAR was in town. Which usually draws a lot of patrons, because the speedway is about five minutes away.

"Hey, Kaid, what's the deal? Tonight you've got a full house,"

Roxy asked, pulling her drumsticks out of the black velvet case she carried them in. We were setting up on the small stage that sat to the right of the bar/ lounge area, with drums, sax, guitars, and a black piano that belonged to the restaurant.

Kaid dressed in Khaki slacks and a navy blue long-sleeve dress shirt of fine silk. His clean-shaven 40-something face with small wrinkles that slightly lined his eyes. He looked distracted today.

"Yeah, it's all because of that press conference earlier, I have camera crews here, reporters, and people from all over the city out to talk about it all, but I can't complain, right, girls?"

We all looked at one another and agreed that more is better in the restaurant biz; slow nights meant fewer tips.

"I just can't stop thinking about it,"

I responded. Still trying to keep the conversation going about Chanel's murder.

Kaid seemed distracted, but he had heard what I said.

"Oh, I'm sorry, did you know the girl who was killed?" he asked.

"Yes, I did, she was a Neighbor, and I had the rotten luck of seeing the body."

"I'm so sorry, Nikki. I heard on the news that she was burned beyond belief."

He shuddered at the thought of what he had just said.

"Sad, just so sad, who would do something like that?" Roxy piped up in the background. We all shook our heads, not knowing really how to respond. Raising our shoulders and giving looks of disbelief at what had occurred went beyond what any of us had ever experienced.

Kaid studied our expressions as if he were trying to see if we knew more than we were letting on. Apparently, I was the only one zeroing in on his behavior, which seemed a little strange for him.

He shrugged his silence off and picked up a pile of mail from the top of the black baby grand piano.

"I have to go, ladies, make sure you get your checks from Donna, she's the Manager tonight. I left them in the safe, and whatever the tips are from the bar, they are to split them with you."

He gave a flirtatious wink and was off.

We started with "The Way You Look Tonight."

The lights were on medium power, and mostly at this time, many families sat for dinner.

The wonderful smells of Filet Mignon and fresh Salmon in butter lingered in the air. The magnificent aroma of garlic, roasted mashed potatoes, and sautéed veggies, creamy clam chowder, and sourdough bread passed by me several times in the evening. Just thinking of the sourdough with salted butter, yum... Now I was hungry, and I wanted to devour food now!

The white linen-covered square and round tables that lined the dining room were all decorated with a small glass vase with a single white rose, Whitewashed antique walls with mahogany wood beams on the ceiling, gave it that old 1930s charm, adding warm lighting and color schemes of navy, ivory, white, and brushed stainless steel fixtures, completed the dazzling simple elegance of this place.

By 7:45 pm it was crowded, we kept the tunes upbeat, singing Mack the Knife, Sway, and Route 66 (which is very fitting here in this town considering we are one block from our main street Foothill Blvd, which is the famous Route 66) Just before we were to take our 1-hour dinner break, none-other than Mayor Grant Mahoney and his wife Veronica Mahoney walked in. They were both dressed in navy suits and were seated in a high booth facing the band. They looked happy; they were smiling and seemed to be in good spirits considering what had happened yesterday, but after what Martin and Oliver had said, these two needed closer attention. Their server brought glasses of water and that scrumptious bread I was still drooling over. She took their order, and they sat calm and quiet. His wife smiled softly and moved closer to him. He seemed quiet and distant, not moving away but just allowing her to be close to him. Weird! I thought.

Dinner break is in the back of the kitchen, with a few mahogany tables with plush chairs in a 250-capacity banquet room.

Generally, it's for banquets or corporate meetings, but during the evening, it's empty, and it is where all of the employees eat their meals. The band had their dinner plates loaded with baked potatoes, salad, and lemon chicken; the steaks and seafood are off limits unless we pay $17.50 per day from our checks. Well, we need all the money we earn, so chicken suits us just fine.

My girls in the band and the servers started talking about dates, makeup, and celeb gossip from TMZ. I was quiet and in deep thought on this case. I know I'm not a detective, but this murder has me unraveled, I have to find out what happened. I began profiling Mayor Mahoney and his wife. They don't look like the kind of couple that would have marital issues; they are both very successful and beautiful and very wealthy, so what gives? Then again, to every family, there are secrets that many people live a lifetime hiding. Maybe they have secrets too!

"What's with you?" Roxy asked as she sat down next to me, her platinum blond hair in a swift French twist.

"Just thinking about Chanel's murder,"

I said, taking small bites of food.

"Well, my money is on an affair with a married lover." Her brown eyes widened in suspense. She held her hands up framing an imaginary image,

" Picture this she has this erotic affair with gentleman X, but then his wife catches the two of them together in the act, gentleman X says *"Oh baby it's not what you think, it didn't mean anything it was just sex."* So wifey loses it, she yells and screams at her husband, *"you piece of no good dog crap!"* she slaps him and he's thrown back but she's not done yet. Oh no, next she runs to the living room, she sees a tall candelabra, and then she strikes poor Chanel on the head, in a fit of rage. Blood gushes out everywhere and her body goes limp, the life rushing out of her, and then gentleman X and the wifey freak out, he yells *"what have you done wife and then she freaks, and then like she says" "It's all your fault,"* then he grabs her and they run off but just before they leave they start a fire with the candle sticks to cover their tracks so that everyone thinks it was just a home fire and then they go on and act like nothing ever happened." At the end of her dramatic story of the events that she believed occurred, the entire room was silent, staff members looked puzzled, and the rest of the band had their jaws dropped.

"What! Like you guys don't think that's what happened!" she said, buttering a roll.
"You really are showing your dark side," I said with my eyebrow arched high, looking slightly in amazement. A tall and very good-looking waiter came by Roxy.

"So are you always like this?" he asked her, devilish and sexy with dark hair and fair-skinned, he looked like Edward Cullen but with more muscle and wild blue eyes.

"You ain't seen nothing yet, baby," she replied. She picked up her plate and walked away to his table to chat and eat. While my Goth best friend, Roxy, and her new Vampire hit it off, I took my plate to the kitchen and stood wondering about the gossip of Chanel moving to another state, did the wife know, and try to put a stop to their plans? If Roxy believed there was a lovers' quarrel, did the police believe it too? When we came back from our dinner break, Tito, one of the bartenders who's been here for many years, gave me a request from a customer.

"Who requested it?" I asked Tito. "Well, I don't know, but there was a note left here at the bar on a cocktail napkin asking the band to play "Someone to Watch Over Me." He said with his strong, tanned arms, shrugging that he didn't know. He reminded me of Dwayne Johnson, aka the Rock. What a cutie he is. "Ok, Tito, whatever the customer wants is fine with me."

he smiled and then said, "Also attached to the napkin was a hundred-dollar bill."

The girls were happy and giggly! We put on our instruments and welcomed ourselves back to the stage, and started playing. I looked out to a packed room, and a familiar face caught my attention, at a booth next to the mayor's booth, a pretty blond in a low-cut black dress sat there with her cosmopolitan cocktail. She was beautiful, and from the looks of it, she knew it! A blond bombshell.

Her date, seated beside her, was handsome and cool. He then smiled a sweet smile, asking for forgiveness or maybe understanding, I couldn't guess. His eyes were warm and kind, filled with so much adornment. I was beginning to tear up. Stop, Nikki, you're a professional, keep your cool. I pushed my feelings aside. Standing tall and grasping the mic, I began, singing to an audience of a full house, the soulful and slightly sultry sound of my voice came through to the audience.

The piano and the sax, and the light drums all collaborated to bring a nice finish to this song. With a cheer of applause, a standing ovation, and one customer even blew me a kiss, away from the eyes of his blond bombshell!

CHAPTER 4

Meeting The Blond Bombshell

I woke up early the next morning, the sun shining and blue skies. I took a cup of Earl Grey out to my patio in my soft plush robe, sitting on a seagrass lawn chair, warm and cozy against the morning chill. My garden of fresh herbs, dry and brittle, begged for my attention. Maybe I needed to bring them inside, I thought. Of course, I am clueless when it comes to gardening. With my eyes closed now, I tried to clear my head of all this week's commotion, but the murder was so fresh in my mind. It kept coming back to me to do all I could to figure out what happened and why Chanel came to such a tragic end.

I felt it was my duty to solve this murder. I had only known Chanel a short time, but she was such a nice girl, and after the things I heard from Martin and Oliver and Jessica, and yes, God forbid Roxy's version of what happened, my passion for justice kept my curiosity fired up.

I knew it was best to leave it to the police, but sometimes there are things that they might miss, right?

Not to mention this complex is my home, the thought of having a murderer among the
neighbors just didn't sit well with me.

No, I had to get involved, at least for the sake of my friends and neighbors.

So far, I had two, no three likely suspects.

1. The bad boyfriend
2. The cheating Mayor
3. The Mayor's wife

Okay, now of course the mayor's wife had a motive. A cheating husband who was going to leave, yeah, of course, any woman would be ready and willing to kill, right?
Next, the boyfriend.

He had a Rap sheet, but what would his motive be? A crime of passion, maybe he found out about Chanel's affair with the mayor and became jealous. Then what about the mayor? Did he mean what he said to Chanel? Maybe she found out he was lying to her, and she threatened to tell his wife.

Would he silence her?
What about his reputation and his political career?
This would be very damaging to everything he's had.
Then maybe she was just in over her head, and they all had a hand in it.
I decided to go out and search for clues...

Later that day, on my way out of the condo, I saw Craig Zane, one of my many neighbors, a schoolmate, and a cop for Rancho Niguel. Most of the time, he works the graveyard shift and exercises during the day, usually doing laps in the pool or benching in the gym. He and I went to the same high school; he used to copy my English test and Math test.

Poor Craig, I'd like to say he made it out of school without my help, but I would be lying to myself.

"Hi, Craig, how has work been lately?"

"Oh, you wouldn't believe how busy we are there, with all that happened with Chanel."
He had a gym bag with his police gear.
"Are you going in to work right now?"

"Yeah, they switched me from graveyard to days. I've also been assigned to help investigate the case," he said with pride. "Oh, Craig, that's great, wow, you got a promotion?"

"Something like that," he brushed it off.
I had the burning question in the back of my mind; I needed to know what Craig knew.
I tried to be discreet, you know, casual conversation.
"So do you guys have any leads right now?"
He scratched his head and started to think about what he was allowed to say. His strong, muscled arms flexed from his grip on the gym bag he was holding.
"Well, not much right now, we have a few good leads but no arrest at this time," he said, beginning to walk away.

"Craig, I'm not the media, you have known me since high school, you used to copy my math test in the 9th grade." he stopped and looked around and said to me, "Why are you so interested?"

"She was a friend." his face softened, and his jaw tightened as if he was wrestling with his mouth to get the words out.

He looked around again then he said

"She knew her killer, there was no forced entry and there were signs of a struggle and sexual assault, plus we found a piece of a metal letter either an N or V, it looks like it fell off a key chain or something like that, look you don't breath a word of this or I'll lock you up myself." he said pointing a strong thick finger at me.

"Ok, Craig, my lips are sealed, I promise," I said, mimicking a lock and key over my mouth.

"I gotta go, expect a call from Kiana." He fished out his keys from his pocket and walked away.

Kiana, Craig's wife, a small size 4 with a kind personality and a job with the city in the planning department, was a good friend to me, but what she saw in Craig, I don't know, maybe it was all body.

Craig walked back to me,

"She's having a candle party next week. Do me a favor and buy a few things from her, be a friend, help her out after all you owe me, nothing is free, Nikki," he laughed.

Oh, crud! I knew that info came with a price.

"You haven't changed since high school, Craig."

He waved and jumped into his new racing royal blue Dodge Challenger and headed out.

I arrived a little early at the Rancho Niguel Community Center. The California bungalow style décor is all the rage in California these days.

The vast real estate in So Cal was largely turn-of-the-century bungalows in Pasadena, LA, and many small valley communities like Claremont, Glendora, Upland, and Monrovia. Once, summer homes to the wealthy and elite East Coasters.

During the turn of the century, many of them headed to Southern California and built small vacation cottages.

Generally, two to three-bedroom style homes with leaded glass windows, built-in china cabinets, and brick fireplaces.

They were located close to all of the hot Los Angeles spots for sports like the Santa Anita race track, the Rose Bowl, and several beaches and gaming locations.

Some of these homes were even used for having many prohibition parties for the rich. The bungalow style was very popular and became a staple of luxury and elegance.

The perfect rendition of these types of homes is made by the Disneyland California Adventure Hotel. For 350+ dollars a day, you can stay with Mickey Mouse in a "bungalow" style room.

The morning sun poured into the lobby from the automatic cherry wood door that opened on command to every person who came to it. I walked down the hall from the lobby to the yoga center room. The soft tan walls and a slight scent of jasmine calmed your nerves when you entered the door.

Jessica, my friend from Starbucks, was already sitting cross-legged with her eyes closed on her purple mat.

I took my pink yoga mat out and laid it next to Jessica. "Hey, what's up?" I asked.

She opened her eyes. "Oh, hi Nikki, how's the investigation going?" she whispered.

"Don't ask, I still have nothing really, just small clues that are making me crazy."

"I don't have anything new either; I've been working so much I haven't had a chance to talk to Blanca."

"We'll just keep your ears open, so many people are involved in this town, we're bound to hear something."

"Yeah, like I heard..." She stopped and looked down as if she had said something she shouldn't have. "Uhh, nothing. I forgot what I was going to say."

"Jessica, tell me?" She was behaving strangely.

"No, I did forget what I was going to say. I guess I just got ahead of myself, anyway," she tousled her dark hair and waved her hand as if to excuse what she was talking about.

I let it go, and we got on the subject of today's workout.

This class is usually filled with many moms getting into their zen during school hours or college kids who have night classes. It's a great workout, and I have to say it's been doing wonders for my thighs. The instructor was ready to begin when two latecomers came quietly into the class and set their mats down in the back of the room. The two girls looked familiar, one redhead and one blond, both dressed in black exercise pants and white tank tops. They came in fast, so I just barely caught a glimpse of them. The redhead, I know her, oh, where have I seen her? The blond I knew her too, she resembled a customer from last night. I thought to myself. Then it hit me right smack in the middle of my downward dog; it came to me. The blond was the girl in the booth next to the mayor; she was the one having dinner last night with Matt.

I cleared my head for now and got into warrior pose, and focused my breathing for complete rejuvenation.

After class, I asked Jessica if she knew who the blond was.

"Oh, that's Summer Simons, she was a good friend of Chanel."

"She's also the one dating Matt, isn't she?"

Jessica covered her mouth with her hand.

"Oh my God, yes, I just didn't want to be the one to tell you."

"It's ok, Jessica, Matt, and I are over. I don't feel bothered by it."

She gave me a look of doubt. "You're not a very good liar, I mean, c'mon, we're talking about hot hunky Matt, the one you're in love with, remember."

"Jessica, we are over. I don't care who he is dating, but I would like to know how and what she knows about Chanel."

"C'mon, I'll introduce you." She wasn't convinced, but she let it go. We picked up our mats and walked over to the blond and the redhead.

"Hi, Summer." Jessica said, casually walking by them,

"Hi Jessica, how's Starbucks?" Summer smiled,

"Busy, as you know."

They gave Beverly Hills hugs (the simple pat on the shoulders, air kisses, and fake smiles).

It was so annoying! Summer then turned to me.

45

"I don't believe I've had the pleasure of personally meeting the famous Nikki Rodriguez."

She said, extending her hand.

"Hi, it's nice to meet you," I said, shaking her hand.

"The same here, I love your band, they're fantastic."

"Thank you." I smiled, accepting her compliment.

I couldn't tell if she was being nice or sarcastic; she seemed harmless, with an honest smile, friendly blue eyes, and long, curly blond hair, like Polly Anna meets Sex In The City. I was really hating her perfection. Worst of all, she was dating my ex, talk about awkward.

Polly Anna (The blond bombshell) turned to her redhead friend, "This is Trixie, my roommate."

I nearly fell over, Trixie! That was the squeaky Barbie that was flirting with Matt yesterday at Sprouts Market when I was getting my sandwich. The one who said Matt, I'm yours with a wink of her eye.

The one that endlessly flirted with him... ugg!!

"Hi, you look familiar, do you work at Sprouts Market in the deli?" Oh yeah, she remembered me, she was still faced, knowing well that I had witnessed her flirting with Matt.

With a slow nod, she said, "Yes, I do, you ordered lunch yesterday at the counter."

"That's right."

I smiled to myself, how would Polly Anna (Miss Summer) like to know that Big Red here, her trusted roommate, was trying to scam her new man? Naughty girl!

I looked Big Red up and down. She wasn't Matt's type by a long shot, too young, too stupid, and too dependent on the desperate attention she demanded, a fake boob job, overly white teeth, a fake tan, a shallow personality, and arrogance. A complete trophy wife wanna-be...At least Matt had taste. I knew he wouldn't go for her.

Jessica spoke up next, "Summer, I just wanted to say how sorry I am about Chanel. You're going to the funeral tomorrow morning, right?"

Summer looked away as if she didn't want to show any emotion.

"Yes, I will be there."

"Were you a close friend of Chanel?" I asked

"Yes, we were very good friends. She was my first roommate when she first came to Rancho Niguel.
We had become great friends. Then she started working for the mayor, and then she bought that condo and then."

Her eyes welled up with tears, and she wiped them away quickly.

"I'm sorry it's still hard for me, I just can't believe that she's gone, but I hope the SOB that did it will fry."

Her tone went from sorrow to anger, her eyes stormy with rage.
Jessica and I exchanged sudden glances.
"Summer, do you have an idea of who might have killed Chanel?"
She pulled a tissue from her backpack and dried her eyes.
The yoga classroom was now empty except for the four of us, she whispered.

"That creep, John Amos." "

CHAPTER 5

Time to Chase Clues

From the long conversation that Summer gave us, it turned out John Amos was a bad boyfriend! Summer and Chanel made numerous calls to the police for disturbing the peace, assault, theft, stealing money and jewelry from her, and even taking their new TV. It seems that Chanel had a restraining order on her ex, and for good reason, too! Summer claimed that John was stalking Chanel; he would follow her everywhere and leave at least 30 messages a day on her answering machine, and he even slept on her doorstep. Talk about scary, but then he was arrested for a burglary charge and got 18 months in prison. After that, Chanel was relieved and started getting her life back together. Summer didn't mention anything about the affair with the mayor,

and I didn't expect her to. From what Martin and Oliver had said, no one knew about it! Summer gave all of this information to the police, and they told her it was helpful and that they would be in touch. I had to ask Craig about it; maybe he would have more info for me. As far as Polly Anna, well, ok, Summer seemed like a smart woman, Someone I probably would have been friends with if she wasn't dating my ex. She was a nice person, not like her scamming friend Big Red. After I showered and dressed, I phoned Oliver and clued him in on what

Summer had told Jessica and me. "You're right, Nikki, he was a bad guy, and from what Chanel told us about him, he fits the mold, but I still think it has to do with the mayor."

"I know Oliver, but maybe it was a crime of passion, maybe John found out about Chanel and Mayor Mahoney."

"Nikki, I have to go. I have Kaid here to pick up his painting. Meet us tonight at CPK for dinner, we'll pow-wow."

"Ok, see you then." I hung up and drove down Route 66 and headed to the city hall building, my air conditioner going full blast and my radio blaring the song of Depeche Mode's "Just Can't Get Enough." I pulled into the parking lot and parked next to a tall maple tree. Plenty of shade, which is good now, maybe the 98 degrees won't swelter my car so badly.

I walked into the police department; the front lobby carried the same bungalow theme as the community center, the room adorned with pictures of city events and posters of the DARE program framed in cherry wood hung on the walls. In a corner was a coffee station, two large thermoses filled with java purchased from Starbucks. I walked up to the officer sitting at a desk behind the counter. The word " RECEPTION " was printed in big burgundy block letters on the wall.

"Good day, ma'am, how can I help you?" a tanned, well-groomed Hispanic deputy asked. He was cute, I almost flirted with him, but then I saw the ring on his finger, Married, all the cute ones always are. I fully break for wedding rings, and that's not negotiable. "Hi, officer, I'd like to speak with Detective Zane."

"Just one moment, ma'am," he went behind the cherry wood partition that was behind him, which likely led to the back office.

While I waited, I walked around the lobby looking at the pictures on the wall until Officer Good-looking came back to the desk.

"Ma'am, I'm sorry Detective Zane is out on a call. Can I take a message?" Disappointed, I thought No, I'll just call him later.

"No, that's ok, it can wait."

"Is there anything I can help you with?" he asked.

I shook my head, "No, thank you."

"Ok, have a nice day."

"Thank you."

He went back to filling out a form and answering the phone that began to ring. Two other women came in behind me and inquired about their stolen car. Well, now that Craig isn't available, I guess I should go and try to find out what the Mayor's office can tell me.

I took my sunglasses out of my purse, ready to bear the bright sunshine and 98 degrees of intense heat. Did I already mention that? When the door to my right opened and exposed officers working diligently at their desks, it looked like the set of a cop show.

Phones rang, sounds of computer keyboards and mice were clicking, and uniformed officers and detectives in suits were busy working hard for the city. The door was held open by a tall detective with dark shades and Levis, it was Detective Anderson. Yay, I did a silent little happy dance!

"Oh, Lois, tell Det. Mc. Kelvie, I'll get back to him later." He said as he was walking out. Obviously, he gave his orders to his plump-looking secretary in a tight-fitting navy blue skirt and matching blazer. Now was my chance to try to talk to him and see if he had anything new. I pretended not to notice him at first, talking on my cell phone as if someone was on the other line. "Okay, bye,"

I said, ending my fake phone call.

I passed by him, trying to bump into him in an accident, and bingo. We both walked into each other.

"Oh, I'm so sorry," I said with honey dripping all over my words. Then, using my sweet smile that made me look foolishly innocent.

"I'm sorry too! I should watch where I'm going." He bent over to pick up his blue-covered cell that fell out of his hand.

"Can I help you with anything?"

"I was just here to see Officer Zane, but he's out on a call."

He put his phone in his back pocket and smiled, "Are you his wife?"

"Oh, Lord, no, Craig and I go way back to high school. I know his wife, I'm friends with her, and we live in the same condo complex."

I had hoped I was coming off sincere and that he didn't have the cop radar turned on high so that he would see right through me. Calm and cool, I finished my story.

"I just needed to ask him if he was going to Chanel's funeral tomorrow. See, I was asking all of the tenants if they wanted to donate money for a large flower arrangement for the church service tomorrow." I said lying so well, but it was a good cover.

I also made a mental note to buy some flowers.

"You're Nikki Rodriguez," he said as if he recognized a big celebrity.

"Yes, how do you know me?" I asked, feeling uneasy now, maybe Craig had told him I was asking about the murder. Crap, now what!

"You're the fireman's girlfriend, the one with the band, I saw you perform last night at Kendal's."

Oh, thank God, he doesn't suspect anything. Wait just a minute, who wasn't at Kendle's last night? Ugh.

How did I not see Detective Good looking there among the sea of people? Oh yeah, maybe because I was wallowing over Matt again, damn that man!

"Ex-girlfriend, we're not together anymore."

"I'm sorry," he said so politely and with relief. I think.

"It's ok, and you are?" I held out my hand to shake his.

"Detective Paul Anderson, you were really good last night. I am a big fan of jazz, and your rendition of "God Bless The Child was fantastic."
He was smiling now.

Oh my God, this guy likes Billie Holiday.

What were the chances? Matt liked Jazz too, but he never remembered who sang what; he just said it was fun to listen to.

"You're a Billie Holiday fan, wow." I said,

"Yeah, my Grandma loved her music, and she used to play her records while she cooked dinner for the family on Sundays." He said, looking me straight in the eyes.

Okay, maybe the clouds were floating away on this one. Detective Anderson and I were hitting it off nicely; he wasn't the tough, rude, crude cop I thought he was. Maybe he just didn't like the press hovering around his investigation.

"It's good to know I have a fan," I said, giving my best smile.

"So you're a tenant in the condos?" his expression wore that of the constant cop, detecting any sign of information that would give him all the answers to the questions he wasn't asking.

"Yes, I am."

"I'm sorry about Ms. O'Connor, but you and the other tenants can bet on the fact that we are doing everything in our power here to give her justice," he said. I felt the sincerity and honesty in his words.

"Thank you, detective, I appreciate your dedication to this case."

"You're welcome," he smiled, then he said,

"Hey, look, I'm on my way out. I have some police business to take care of, but maybe I can catch another show of yours, and we could have a drink."

He was asking me out, oh man, I hope I'm not blushing, obviously, I wear my heart on my sleeve, and now if I were the color of red tomatoes, he would know just how flattered I actually was. Then another thought hit me fast, this is a good thing, I get to know him, he gets comfortable with me, he shares info with me, he's cute too, this is exactly what I was looking for.

I looked into his blue/green eyes and felt myself go limp. Earth to

Nikki, wake up, stupid. My inner voice of reason is shaking me!!!

"Yeah, that would be great. I'm performing on Friday night at Kendle's again. Come by about 7 pm, and I'll have a table reserved for you.

"All right, I'll be there, it's a date."

"See you on Friday." I waved and walked out to the car I could tell he was watching me. I put the car in reverse and headed off.

That night after practice, I went across the street to get some dinner. I had invited Roxy, but she had a date with the Vampire waiter from Kendle's. I was meeting Oliver and Martin at CPK, and I was craving a Waldorf salad and a glass of Pinot Grigio. My black strap heels clicked on the cobblestone floor beneath me as I tried to run, not walk, across the way to the mall. The summer air was cool, finally, and I was glad I had remembered to bring my white cotton wrap that went beautifully with my new black and white crepe summer dress.

I just loved it when White House/Black Market had a sale on their dresses; it wouldn't set me back in my savings account, so why not?

CPK, otherwise known as California Pizza Kitchen, was busy this evening. Martin and Oliver looked dashing in their long-sleeved dress shirts and silk ties. "Over here, Nikki," they beckoned.

I slid into the high-back booth that faced the open kitchen and the entire restaurant.

"Oh, Nikki, you look fabulous, girl!" Oliver said and sipped his chardonnay. "Thanks, it's new!" I said, opening a menu.

"Well, you do look great, but I have news for you," Martin said, as he took a long drink of his Samuel Adams. Then he moved in close to

Oliver, and I like it was a secret only meant for our ears. "The police caught John Amos!" He took another drink of his beer and sat back, satisfied with filling us in on the latest.

"How did you find out?" I asked, but then we were interrupted by our server.

"Hello, my name is Jade. I'll be your server this evening. What can I get you to drink?" I was still in shock at what Martin had just said. "Uhh, yes of course, how about a Lavender martini."
I said, ordering something stronger than the Pinot Grigio that I'd had in mind. The young twenty-something server smiled her 40-watt smile and bleached white teeth. "Oh, those are my favorite too. I'll be right back to take your order as well," she said, and she was off.

"Ok, Martin, spill it, how did you find out, and how come you didn't tell me earlier?" Oliver spat out.
"Look, I just found out an hour ago myself, I had to go the bank to make our deposit for the gallery like I do every other day, and on my way, you know how you have to pass the Police sub-station in the mall before you reach the parking structure, ok well I'm walking by the sub-station and then that detective Anderson, the one that's heading up Chanel's murder investigation." We nodded

"Well, I see him walking out of the sub-station with two other Uniformed cops and a real hard-looking guy in cuffs.

Then he puts him in the car and tells the other two officers, "Yeah, that's him, that's the guy we've been looking for, that's John Amos."

"What did he look like?" Oliver asked. He had taken the words right out of my mouth; that was for sure.

"He was about six feet tall, early 30s, with dark long hair, tattoos, and dressed like a biker from the old school days, not like the yuppie baby boomers you see riding Harleys today, in their designer chaps and Calvin Klein leather jackets, no, this one was a real badass."

Jade had come back with my drink, and she took our order. I waited until she was gone to spill it all. I smiled like a chest shire cat and told them about my plans. "Well, I've got some news of my own, I've got a date with Detective Anderson," I said, taking a sip of my drink.

"No way, Nikki. When did this happen?"

I filled Martin and Oliver in on how I squared the date off with Detective Anderson, and then we discussed what I had learned from Summer this morning.

"Well, Summer may think John Amos is the one who did it, but I still say it was someone else," Martin said.

"I don't know Martin having a stalker like Amos, it definitely points to a crime of passion, the guy wouldn't leave her alone, she had a restraining order on him, and what about the stealing and the abuse? I think it's like all those movies on the Lifetime channel, he just fits the mold."

"So you think that he believed if he couldn't be with her, then no one could." Oliver asked,

"Yeah, I mean, think about it, she was trading up in every way, her home, her job, and of course, her man, John Amos had to know about the Mayor or at least that she had a man in her life."

"No, Nikki, Chanel was very careful about being with Mayor Mahoney. I don't think John would have known."

"Somebody other than you two knew, now we need to know who!" After dinner, we walked back to the condos and decided to call it a night. Martin and Oliver walked me to my door.

"So are you two going to the funeral on Friday?"

"We'll be there, we have our part-timer to cover the gallery while we're gone."

"Well, get ready for another media frenzy in this town tomorrow."

"Yep," we had all agreed.

"Thanks for walking me home."

"No problem at all."

"Oh yeah, Nikki, I almost forgot, I saw Matt earlier today," Martin said.

"Yeah, was Summer glued to his arm?"

"No, he was alone, he was selling tickets for the pancake breakfast, and he wanted to know if we could donate an art piece for the auction next month, and he asked me how you were doing."

Martin was treading carefully in the waters of the big breakup I had; he was concerned for us. We were all friends, and of course, friends never wanted to see their good friends break up or be sad.

"He knows my number and where I live."

"He also said he misses you." He said quietly, waiting for my reaction. I rolled my eyes,

"Really, he seems to have moved on with Summer."

Martin put his arm around my shoulders for a brotherly hug.

"I'm not so sure about that, Nikki." They were sweet for being so optimistic with Matt and me, but seriously, it was over.

"Good night, guys." Martin and Oliver headed to their condo, and I safely locked the deadbolt behind me!

CHAPTER 6

The Funeral

I woke up early after a night of tossing and turning. My mind was racing with images of John Amos and Detective Anderson, who were arguing over the line of questioning about Chanel's murder. At one point in the dream, Chanel herself was questioning John, demanding to know why he killed her. Her face was full of blood, and her blond hair was matted with leaves and dirt. She was cursing him! Then Detective Anderson joined her in beating John Amos until his tattooed arms could no longer pick himself up. Then Matt came into the dream, he was wearing his fireman blues uniform and carrying an ax. He came running into the interrogation room and demanded that Detective Anderson release the man. In the middle of this commotion, the police department changed, and now everyone was in my condo living room, and Matt and Detective Anderson were arguing over me. I tried to tell them to stop, but then Chanel came in and shot both of them, and then she looked at me through blood-red eyes and said, "Now you can't choose any of them, they're dead just like me!"

I screamed and screamed until my eyes flew open and I woke up in my own bed. My pink cotton baby doll nightgown was damp from all the sweat coming down my back.

It was a nightmare, just a dream. For several moments, I sat in bed thinking that maybe Chanel was trying to tell me something, contacting me from the other side. What it probably meant was that I had too much on my mind, and maybe that Lavender Martini was creeping back up!

It was 7:34 am, so I turned on the tube to Channel 5 to see if there was any news on the arrest of John Amos.

Sure enough, the news was reporting from the Rancho Niguel police department about the arrest that was made yesterday. According to the report, John had been brought in for questioning, but since he had violated his parole, he had been arrested and would be in jail until his trial. Police would not comment on whether or not they had any evidence of John being involved with his deceased ex-girlfriend's murder; police said it was still an ongoing investigation.

I turned off the TV and went in for a shower.

Funerals are always so creepy, the sad, dreary church music that's piped out by an ancient organ, or the doomed march that plays when the pallbearers carry the casket out. Anyway, I arrived at St. Mark's Catholic Church on time, and there were so many people that you would have thought some celebrity had just died. News reporters, city people, the Mayor's office, business owners, and even more news reporters circulated outside St Mark's parking lot.

I spotted Martin and Oliver sitting in the seventh pew from the left. "Hi, guys," I whispered. "Hi Nikki," they said and hugged me. "Sit here with us," Oliver said, making room in the pew.

"So what do you make of all these people?" I asked just in a dim whisper.

"I think it's for political reasons; none of them really cared for poor Chanel," Martin said as he watched all the faces walking up to the casket. The church was adorned with large flower pieces, some tall, some round, and even some on the walls. The colors of white, pink, and pale yellow lay on the white casket. "So, are you ready to get in line, Nikki, so we can say one last goodbye?" Oliver was starting to tear up; a silk navy blue handkerchief in his hand matched the navy blue tie he wore over his starched white dress shirt. "You mean to go up there to the casket." I turned green!!! Here was my freaking out part of funerals, Martin and Oliver must have seen the look on my face because they said in unison. "We'll be right by your side."

"Don't worry, it's not an open casket, Nikki. " Oliver said.

I lifted my chin and spoke,

"I'll be fine, I just need a minute, but you guys go ahead."

They nodded and went ahead to join the massive line of mourners who were crying and marching to the casket.

I sat down and tried to calm my nerves. I looked around the church to see who would be sitting in the family section of pews.

I didn't remember hearing about Chanel's mother and father, but there was a couple that looked to be in their mid-sixties. The woman had blond/grey hair and features that resembled Chanel's. The gentleman had a kind, sincere face that was red and blotchy, most likely from crying.

I watched Mayor Mahoney and his wife shake their hands and offer condolences to them.

The look on Mrs. Mahoney's face was stern and raw, her eyes were cold and gray, Mayor Mahoney had red blotches around his eyes, and he was, for once, not so suave; his manner showed his distraught emotion.

I spotted Summer walking back to her seat with Matt on her arm. Her tears were streaming, but she kept her cool. Mrs. Green was in the fourth pew from the front, dabbing at her eyes.

I had finally worked up the nerve to go up to the casket and pay my last respects to Chanel. The line was smaller now, and my view of the casket was closing upon me.

I slowly walked to the closed casket that held a 10x10 framed picture of Chanel. Because of the condition of her body, there was no way they would have had an open casket.

Mrs. Green came beside me, crying and saying, "She was such a sweet girl." She did look sweet in the picture; the make-up was soft, and her hair was curled around her smiling face like Shirley Temple.

"Goodbye, Chanel, I hope Justice finds you soon," I said and returned to my seat.

The ceremony was short, and the burial was even shorter; many of the same people were there from the church as well. The media was told to stay out of the cemetery for privacy and respect to the family and friends of the deceased.

The only new person I saw here that I didn't see at the church was Kaid Kendle. I thought Kaid didn't know Chanel. A few days ago, when the band and I were talking about Chanel's death, Kaid had mentioned that he didn't know her, yet here he was. After the body was lowered to the grave, many people started to leave.

I wanted to stay as long as Kaid was here. I wanted to know why he was here!

He walked by the casket and lingered for a moment; then he tossed a crimson (at least I think it was crimson, although it looked black) long-stemmed rose.

(For those of you who are wondering, I did get a wreath of white and yellow roses for Chanel from all the tenants of the Condo complex, you thought I forgot.)

CHAPTER 7

A Date With a Cop

It was 6:30 pm, and we were setting up for this evening's gig at Kendle's. The hot summer air hung low, like a fog, sticky and sweaty. It seemed like even the air conditioning couldn't keep me cool. My lightweight cotton off-the-shoulder black wrap dress was not doing its job of keeping me cool. I fanned myself with my Japanese rice paper fan, but no cool air came from it. I was excited that I would be meeting Detective Anderson tonight. I was also very curious why Kaid had been at Chanel's funeral; what was he hiding? Kaid's Silver Lamborghini was parked out in front, so I knew he was here. I had to talk to him! "Hey guys, I'm going to go find Kaid. I have a question I need to ask him. I'll be right back."

I told the band as they were setting up, and I went into the kitchen. The staff was busy chopping, cooking, and sautéing vegetables; the smells were heavenly; garlic bread fresh from the oven pierced my stomach, and small growls cried in pain.

Kaid's office was off the kitchen and upstairs, by way of a private staircase to a loft room with a small lobby area. An Asian-style rice paper shade divided the room from the lobby to the office to create a professional look.

The Asian theme was abundant, beautiful silk fabrics adorned the cherry wood chairs and the large chaise.

A huge white fan with cherry blossoms on it hung on the wall, above a reception desk; pieces of jade artwork filled the two-story cherry wood bookcases. A small water fountain spilling water over a black carving of stone stood in a corner. I had been up here several times, and still, it was beautiful when I reached the top of the stairs. The office was dark except for a small lamp in Kaid's office, where I heard some whispering.

"I told you I would take care of it, and I did. Now don't call me here again, I'll meet you later, now stay focused, and don't blow it." The phone slammed down, and then I heard footsteps. I ran behind the lobby front desk and crouched under it to hide.

Kaid walked from around the divider, turned off the lamp, and walked to the staircase to head to the kitchen. When the coast was clear, I crawled out from the desk.

Weird, who was he talking to, and what was it that someone was going to blow? I walked around the divider into Kaid's office; I turned on the lamp on the large black desk. I saw invoices for the restaurant, M&M Produce, Thor's Meats, and Kamikaze Liquor.

I opened the desk drawer, and nothing but pens and pencils, highlighters, and paper clips were all neatly organized in a desk tray.

I opened a few of the file cabinets, employee forms,

Copies of tax stuff, invoices and a checkbook, and payroll files.

Nothing unusual there. I tried the very last drawer of the large black file cabinet, but it was locked. I opened the desk drawer and searched for a key. I looked under the tray, and there it was, a small gold key.

I turned the key, and bingo, the file cabinet opened.

Only one file was in the cabinet; it was labeled

R.I.

I opened it up, curious as to what R.I. would stand for.

There was a bank book from the 1st. Bank of Nassau

had a balance of $ 300 million dollars under the name of

Jack Mendel. Who is Jack Mendel? I thought, puzzled even more now.

Why does Kaid have someone's financial information? I heard some

voices coming from the stairs, and I put everything back.

My heart racing now, the momentum of this cat spying was giving me

the cardio workout that I had missed this morning.

"Kaid, the caviar is spoiled. I need a new crate of it by 12 noon

tomorrow if we're going to have it for the mayor's dinner that we're

catering."

"Don't worry, Pierre, we'll have it, I'll give you cash, and you can call

Chef Spirion at St. Gerard's, he has a special reserve for me."

"Magnific, you are the best boss any chef could ask for, Masseur

Kendle," the chef said in a mock French accent.

They went into Kaid's office, and I had time to get out of there.

I hid out in the hall of the kitchen, grabbed a piece of garlic bread, and

started munching. Kaid and Chef wannabe French came down the

staircase. "Nikki, what are you doing back here?"

I thought fast... "Oh my God, this is the best garlic bread I have ever

had. I just had to snatch a piece," I said, closing my

eyes and making mmmm sounds.

Kaid just smiled and said, "No problem, eat as much as you like, butterfly, just don't go ruining that figure," he said and walked with the chef to the front of the kitchen.

My eyes narrowed at his sexist comment, what a douche...

Little Black Dress always brings out a large number of people, and tonight was no exception. The two-hour wait was giving our tip jar a nice green look to it. We took a few requests, "Blue Moon" for a group of 1950s guests who were on their way to Palm Springs for their 1959 high school reunion. A young couple from Pasadena requested "Still The One" from Shania Twain, and a bowling team from Covina requested "Born To Be Wild."

At 7 pm sharp to the old tune "The Best Is Yet To Come."

Detective Anderson walked in, dressed in a pair of dark jeans, a black short-sleeved shirt, and snake-skin cowboy boots. Yummy...
"Thank you very much, ladies and gentlemen. We're now going to take a break, but we'll be back in 15 minutes."

The house music went on, and we all put down our instruments and went to the bar, except for me; I made my way to the reserved table for Detective Anderson and me.
"You were fantastic."

"Oh, thank you, it pays the bills."

"You ever think of cutting a record?"

"Yes, maybe someday."

We ordered drinks, a beer for him and a Coke for me. I was still on duty, so no liquor. Yet!

"So tell me, how did you sneak away with all of this investigating you're so busy with?"

"I have a lot of people helping me, that's how."

His smile was sweet, his handsome face mature and yet boyish. I wondered what kind of man lurked behind the mysterious green/bluish eyes; they casually fell to view the plunging neckline of my black dress.

"I see," I said, smiling.

"So, tell me, Detective Anderson, do you...

"Please call me Paul."

"Ok, Paul, do you enjoy police work?"

"I do, I enjoy giving people justice, and it makes me feel like I'm giving someone a feeling of relief over their pain."

"I guess it leaves little time for a social life, right?"

"Yes, it does."

"So are you a local here?"

"No, I grew up in Pasadena. I started my career at LAPD. I was there for five years, and I decided I needed a change. So here I am. I've been a resident for two months now."

"LAPD, wow, I'm sure you were never bored there."

"Yes, you can say that."

"What do you do when you're not at work?"

"I like to go surfing,"

Bingo!!! Give the lady a stuffed animal. Was I right about the surfer thing?

"I enjoy Kayaking, canoeing, camping, swimming, and I play basketball with some friends on Sunday afternoons. Poker nights once a month on Thursdays."

"Guy's stuff I see."

"You can say that, although it would be nice to do something new. What are your hobbies?"

"Well, you already know I sing, and hmm, let's see, I like to lie on the beach and read a good mystery novel, or I like to do Yoga and go for a run, I play tennis on Sundays and at some point, I intend to see Paris, but for now I'm saving my money for retirement."

"What, no husband, kids, and a house in the suburbs?" he asked in a joking manner.

"I'm taking my time with all of that, I'm not really the type of girl that's ready to commit, there's just so much to do."

"I couldn't agree more, it's nice to finally date someone who just wants to go out and get to know each other instead of pulling me to the altar after the third date."

"No way have you actually had someone do that to you."

"Just about."

"Well, you have nothing to worry about. I don't want to marry you," I teased.

I took a look at my Gucci watch."Looks like break time is over, I'll be

69

just another hour, and then we can have a bite to eat."

"Sure."

"Okay, do you have a special request?"

He thought for a moment,

"How about something from Sinatra?"

"Okay, you got it."

After our last song, I helped the girls pack away the band equipment and put it in the red Dodge minivan we called Beulah.

"Goodnight, girls," I said, heading back into Kendal's

Roxy was walking to her car, shaking her head as if she just couldn't believe what she was seeing.

"So is this on the level, you dating a cop?" Roxy asked, trying to read me.

"He's nice, I like him."

"You and men in uniform, what is it with you?"

"I ... I think he might be good for me, you know," I said, trailing my words off and looking down at my non-manicured hands.

"What about hero man, Matt?"

"He's dating someone else, he's over me, so why can't I move on to?"

"As long as you're happy, then Roxy is happy too."

"Why is Roxy talking about herself in the third person again?"

"Oh, you know me, always the attention hog, I like martyring myself."
She smiled, gave me a big hug, and slid into her car.

"Be good, and call me later, I want details," she drove away in her black 1969 Camaro. Detective Anderson sat at a high booth with a large window that looked out to the bustling streets of the outdoor mall.

"So are you ready to order?" I asked, sliding in next to him.

"Yeah, what do you recommend?"

"Anything, the food here is great, try the filet mignon with sautéed mushrooms in brandy sauce, it's incredible."

"Okay, I think I will."

"I have a question for you," I knew I had to be subtle; I didn't want him to think even for one moment I was snooping into his investigation. "How would you know if you have a good lead on a suspect? I mean, so you don't arrest the wrong person."

He thought for a moment as if he was trying to figure out why I would ask him.

"You don't really want to know this, do you?"

"Of course, I want to know what your day is really like,"

He smiled confidently.

"Really, this is great, you're the only date I've had that wanted to talk shop." he was flattered, and yes, my plan went into motion

Ladies rule 1. To get your subject to talk, bring up what he is good at. Men like to talk about what they know. It's good to get them blabbing, and then they drop the wall and really let you in.

"So here's the thing: we have to have evidence that will put the suspect at the time of the murder or crime, and we have to have a weapon or a piece of DNA; the evidence has to be solid, or else we don't have a case. The DA won't accept it if he or she can't have solid evidence. Nowadays, with all the technology we have, it makes our job a little easier."

"So do you have DNA or a weapon every time you arrest a person?" I asked

"Well, it varies from case to case, you know, for domestic disturbances we have the spouse or witnesses, but for let's say a murder case, we need hard evidence, surveillance of the crime, witnesses, a weapon, or maybe something that puts the person in the time or place of the murder. In order to prosecute, we can't arrest on suspicion of murder even if the cards all point to the person. We do have to make sure our job is thorough."

Our dinner arrived, but we continued to talk about police work, and believe it or not, I was very interested.

"So this case you're working on right now, is it in the bag, so to speak?" I asked casually, making it seem like it didn't matter whether or not he gave me the answer, even though it was burning in me to know the truth.

He cleared his throat and leaned in a little closer to me. "I'm not at liberty to discuss any part of the case, but let's just say that I need to be convinced with all of the evidence I have," he said quietly.

I guess I was on the right track; he knew something was missing, too.

"You know I have to be honest with you, Paul, from what the papers and the news said, it seems like this Amos character is the right guy."

"Yes, it does, but just remember one thing: not everyone is who you think they are." That piece of advice would help me later, and I would refer to it as more than just a philosophical phrase.

After dinner, Paul walked me to my door.
"I had a great time this evening. It was nice getting to know you."

I said, taking my keys out of my clutch bag.
"Thank you, I had a great time too," he said.
I turned the lock on the door, I felt his breath on my neck, and it gave me chills.

"So maybe I'll run into you again, Paul, and we can try canoeing or kayaking."

"That would be fun, you would love it.

"I'm sure I would."
We were standing very close now, and I knew any moment we would say goodbye with a kiss.
Of course, as luck would have it! His phone went off.
He pulled it out of his pocket.

"Sorry, I've got to take this," he held up his finger, asking for just one minute.
Then answered his phone,
"What's going on?"

He asked.
Obviously, this wasn't good news.

His jaw tightened, and the muscles in his arms were flexing with anger.

"I'll be there in five minutes!"

"What's wrong?" I asked,

"John Amos is dead."

CHAPTER 8

Case Closed

The sun shone bright in the kitchen, gleaming stainless steel reflections from the French press danced on the wall, the sweet aroma of Kenyan coffee filled my nose, and the birds outside sang a soft chirping lullaby. (No, not really, but it sounded good.) What can I say after last night's news of the death of John Amos?

I began to wonder if he was the killer.

I took my coffee out to the patio, with a small journal that I usually kept under my mattress. I wanted to try and sort out all of the clues I had collected from the big case.
I opened my notebook to the notes I had scribbled down. It seemed so easy to put together at first, but now my theories seem off in some way.

Missing pieces of this puzzle were making me doubt what I had originally thought about the crime.

So, looking at my clues and in no particular order, I went over them again in my mind, and put it together, I thought.

<u>CLUES!</u>

R.I. file in Kaid's file cabinet

Piece of a letter found at the scene of the crime

The arrest of John Amos

Kaid at the funeral for Chanel

Kaid's bizarre conversation with whom?

John Amos' death

But what does Kaid have to do with the murder? Kaid has a successful business here and in Palm Springs.

Why risk his investments?

Is he involved in killing Chanel, and why?

Does he know who killed Chanel?

Did he know Amos? Was Kaid ever in prison?

Did he really make his money from software in Silicon Valley?

Is he shady with a past?

All these questions were still unanswered, and my curiosity was even more amped up than before.

Today, it was all over town, the death of John Amos sent all the news media here again, and it was like Barnum and Bailey's circus of news folks.

Starbucks was so packed the line was out the door, and Jessica could only take my Chai tea latte order and say, "See you in yoga class." She was leaving for Palm Springs in two hours, so I wouldn't be able to talk to her later.

I headed to City Hall for the press conference; they had a new setup in the courtyard of the building. A tall podium and some chairs graced the slate patio; people were setting up and checking mics and fastening cords to audio devices.

There were two sections of chairs being put out for members of the city hall board that had paper signs with their names on them. More security, more cops everywhere. The two eucalyptus trees provided filtered shade for the patio, and a small breeze blew through the leaves. I spotted my old pall officer, Craig Zane, and walked up to him to see if he had any new info on John Amos.

"Hey, Craig, I heard what happened, so is this a sign that the killer is still out there?"
He put on his sports coat, and repositioned his Ray Ban Aviator sunglasses (hence a la Tom Cruise from Top Gun), in no way does he look like him!! But now that he was an official detective, he had to look professional.

"Nikki, I can't tell you anything."

"But this does change everything, right? The killer is still out there?"

"Nikki, I'm sorry the case is now going to be officially closed."

"What!"
He looked around to make sure no reporters were listening to our conversation and pulled me toward the glass windows that lined the building. Once he thought the coast was clear, he spilled the info.
"Look, the DA said that since John Amos committed suicide and also because he confessed to the crime, the case is closed."

"But what confession? And how did he kill himself?"

"He gave another inmate a pack of smokes for a shank and stabbed himself in the heart, just after he wrote a note confessing his crime, it's over, Nikki."

"What do you think, Craig?"

"It doesn't matter what I think, case closed," he clapped his hands together to mimic a door closing.

"You know, I think Detective Anderson felt that he wasn't the murderer?"

"Look, Nikki, I know how important this is for you to find justice for Chanel; she was my friend, too, but the facts are the facts, and you have to accept it. She was in an abusive relationship, and even though she got out, it still came back to her." He looked me over with curiosity, now his brief sincerity taking a back seat. "I hope you weren't trying to get info from Anderson; he's not easily fooled." Searching for my reaction for an answer to his question.

"You think I just went out with him to get info on this case?"

"I know you, Nikki, I'm not too far off, am I?" He confessed, telling me with his sly upraised eyebrow that I couldn't pull one over on him.

"Now I can't even date a guy, who are you, my father?"

Hands on his hips, he stood his full size of 6'3 brooding over me, waiting for my response.

"Now that I think about it, Hell, you two are made for each other."

He laughed, "I've got to go, Nikki, remember tonight's candle party at my place, Kiana is expecting you." He ran off.

What a schmuck ... Damn, how does he do that? For some people, it's so easy to get them to do something, and Craig is a pro.

The press conference confirmed what Craig had told me: it was a shank to the heart and a note confessing the crime in detail, but the police did not discuss all that the note said.

I knew still something wasn't right. I would find the answer to this, even if I did have to sweet-talk Officer Anderson.

I was running late for Kiana's candle party. After the press conference, I grabbed my brown rice and chicken ginger broccoli at Pei Wei, an Asian restaurant across from the City Hall that was ahh... amazing.

Then I raced off to get a pair of red flats to go with my denim Capri's and red halter top. I knew I'd probably be spending a fortune tonight, as the trade of favors for the info Craig was giving me. Total shyster!

With my red clutch purse tightly under my arm and my keys in hand, I ran up to the third floor to Craig and Kiana's condo, in building C34.

Their balcony was just across from Chanel's condo in building D. Creepy, I know!

I knocked on the door while putting on my silver hoop earring. Boy, was I always fashionably late! "Hi, Nikki, I'm so glad you made it, honey," Kiana said, opening the door and pulling me in.

Her small size 4 frame was silhouetted with a short pink halter dress.

"Now, Craig said you had a list of things you wanted to buy, oh, thanks, Nikki."

She gave me a light hug.

A list! I was going to kill Craig; now he was pushing it. Instead, I smiled through gritted teeth, "You're welcome, Kiana." Classical music played, while the central air kicked into high gear, and ladies all around me were chatting about candles and furniture. "Can I get you a drink, Nikki?"

"Sure, how about a Coke?"

"Ok, be right back."

I looked around the room, and a long table was set in front of the fireplace, covered with candles of all sizes and colors. Crystal holders, ceramic holders, pillars, and votive holders, just how much was this stuff going to set me back?

I searched around and spotted Summer in a blue tank top and white flare jeans, talking to Big Red, her roommate, in a full-length fuchsia top. She looked at me and glared, and so did Big Red, and they turned and headed to the dining area.

What the heck did I do to her? Stranger things were happening in this town; that vacation of mine is long overdue.

I went over to the buffet table that had hors d'oeuvres of crudités and fresh fruit, cheese cubes, and a chocolate fondue with marshmallows, pretzels, strawberries, and apples.

The strawberries had my name on them.

"Here you are, Nikki."

Kiana said, handing me a Coke in a pink pastel glass,

"Thank you."

She looked winded but very excited, entertaining was quite a workout.

"I invited Roxy, but she said she couldn't make it, and Jessica is in Palm Springs, and Mrs. Green is on a double shift tonight, so I guess this is it, 25 people."

She looked nervous as she twisted her hands back and forth and let out a long sigh.

"You're going to be fine, take deep breaths," I said

She exhaled deeply,

"You're right, I'm fine."

"Kiana," a woman in a Hawaiian print dress called out,

"Gotta go, Nikki." Kiana walked off.

The Hawaiian print dress lady walked to the front of the living room, with Kiana right behind her.

"Okay, ladies, gather round, it's time to start." Clapping her hands to get everyone's attention, all the women in the room took seats, including me.

"My name is Tami, and I represent American Lite, the best candle in America. I am the representative for all of the Rancho Niguel and Riverside region, and you are all here tonight for Kiana to help her launch her new part-time business as your American Lite consultant." There was a round of applause. Kiana went to the front of her living room, and Tami stepped back to let her have center stage.

"Thank you, everyone, for coming tonight. I am excited to be launching American Lite, and I hope you all buy lots of candles." Applause, applause!

We were all handed catalogs of full-color pictures that displayed candles of every shade and every scent known to man.

I skimmed the pages and decided on a nice array of iced teaberry votive candles with crystal glass votive holders that resembled wine glasses. These would be perfect for my long, luxurious bubble baths. I also bought a few large pillar candles for the living room in strawberry lemonade scent and a few packs of tea lights. ok, it set me back about $180 bucks, Craig better appreciate it.

Everyone in the room was putting in orders and taking out their checkbooks. A woman in a long muumuu dress of yellow sat next to me, attaching sticky notes to flag the pages of merchandise she wanted when she turned to me and said: "You know this candelabra was the exact one that poor Chanel had in her home." She caught my attention.

"Did you know her? I mean, how did you know her?" I asked the lady in Yellow. She looked up from her catalog, her thick eyelashes fluttered, and her many gold bangle bracelets jangled as she set her checkbook on her lap. Short curly hair and all she looked like Mrs. Roper from the 1970s show Three's Company.

"Of course, I knew her, I worked with her at City Hall, I'm Marge, one of the secretaries in the office," she said, shaking my hand.

I kept my cool. "I'm Nikki Rodriguez, a friend of hers from the complex here, so you knew her very well?"

Marge put her thick glasses closer to her eyes and took a sip of her punch. "I knew her well, that poor dear, she was so young and so full of life, she was so in love too."

Now that really caught my attention.

I played it off like I knew what she was talking about

"Oh yeah, I remember she mentioned she was seeing someone, but I didn't get his name?" I said,

"Well, dear, she didn't mention his name to me, but she was making plans to leave."

"I thought she loved her job."

"Oh, she did, but she had told me once that it was time to move on and that her fella wanted to move out of state. She said he had a difficult marriage and just wanted a new start." Marge took off her bifocals and rubbed her eyes.

"Yes, she had so many wonderful plans, just a tragedy. I just hope she is

now at peace with the lord."

"The fella, did she say what he did for a living?"

I asked, trying not to sound too hopeful.

"All she said was that he was an older man and that he was going to marry her."

CHAPTER 9

A Sleuthing I Go

That night, I lay in bed thinking about what Marge had said.
An older man, moving away and marriage. If John Amos did murder
Chanel, then why? The note he left only apologized for what he did, not
why. I needed to talk to Kaid. What did he have to do with going to the
funeral? I rolled over, 12:30 am, the round silver clock on my

nightstand read. I couldn't sleep.

I heard all kinds of sounds outside my window: the motorcycles
charging down the street, a few horns honking, an ambulance with
blaring sirens, and a fire truck. Then my phone rang!
OMG, who is crazy enough to call me at this hour?
I picked up the silver old-fashioned style phone with a cord (yes, a
landline)that I had purchased at my favorite store, Pottery Barn, in the
mall. "Hello," I said, sitting up in bed.

"Hi, Nikki, I'm so sorry for calling sooooo... late, but I had to tell you

this before I'm too drunk to remember tomorrow. I'm here in Palm

Springs and my friends and I went to this restaurant and it's the one that

Kaid owns, anyway, I talked to the bartender Brandon and he's an old

high school friend of mine and I asked him if he knew Chanel O'

Conner and he said that he remembers Kaid bringing her to Palm

Springs, he said they stayed at the Ritz Carlton for the weekend."

I jumped out of bed. "Jessica, are you saying that Kaid and Chanel were an item?"

"I don't know, but listen to this, it gets even stranger. Brandon said that the whole weekend, Kaid was at the restaurant managing. He said that Chanel had come into the restaurant for dinner and then went back to her hotel alone; she even told the waitress that she was meeting someone later, not Kaid. Talk about weird."

"Thanks, Jess, for the info. I'll see what I can find out from here." "All right, got to go!"
Click.

After the phone call, I was wide awake, all I could think about was why did Kaid and Chanel have this connection, and who was Chanel going to meet? The mayor? What did all of it mean?
I got up and put on a pair of jeans and a navy blue pullover. I put on my slip-on Nikes and my cell phone in my back pocket and headed out the door.
The complex was quiet and motionless as I walked to building D.
I climbed the stairs quietly and headed for D-24.
The yellow tape was gone, and all that was left on the door was a

bright fluorescent pink notice stating POLICE CRIME SCENE NO ADMITTANCE AT THIS TIME.
I tried the credit card trick and tried to pry the door open that way, but no luck. Our building had great deadbolts, and I guess I should have known that. Rats now what!!

I had to get inside and search for something that could give me a solid lead on this whole mess.

Think Nikki, I looked around the courtyard, potted plants in large red clay pots about the height and size of a small boulder, the kind they sell for a fortune at the local nurseries, but you can get them cheap in Tijuana.

The straw welcome mat in front of the door seemed like a good place to keep a spare key. But no such luck.
I decided to check the pots. I felt around in the damp soil for a few minutes, only to turn up a rolly polly and a cigarette. Hmm, Virginia Slims, I didn't know Chanel smoked.

I was about ready to give up when I thought. How about under the pot? Obviously, it was too heavy or too big to move, so I put all of my weight on it and moved it an inch. The slight scraping noise from the large pot wasn't enough to get any of the other tenants' attention because no one's lights came on.

I looked around the courtyard, trying to detect any movement from windows, but just shadows danced on the walls from the many trees that were blowing in the slight breeze. I looked down to see a shiny gold key. I picked it up and thanked my lucky stars, then I went and tried the lock.

It clicked, and slowly and quietly I turned the knob and crept in. I locked the deadbolt and put the key in my pocket.
I took out the mini mag light that I keep on my key chain, and I searched the room. The room smelled musty and smoky, the ceiling of the condo was under construction, and a large blue tarp sat above new wood beams in the living room. The carpet was still here, stains of burnt furniture and wood shavings covered the floor. The kitchen was

stripped of all of the appliances, and the hardwood floors were down to the floorboards.

I headed to the bedroom, even though it was not damaged by the fire, it still smelled of mold and dampness.
The furniture from her bed to her dresser was gone, and all that remained was a closet full of clothes, untouched and unharmed. I decided to start with the closet, a large walk-in that was standard in all of the condos.

There were several suits, pants, skirts, and silk tank tops from Anne Taylor, some St. Johns from Nordstrom, along with some Betsy Johnson and Lilly Pulitzer pieces. Also, a hefty double rack of shoes, Jimmy Choo's, Prada, Ferragamo, and Manolo Blahnik. Be still, my heart. She definitely had style. I searched her many designer handbags, including Gucci, Dooney and Bourke, Coach, and of course, Prada. They were all empty.
I was at the end of the closet, looking through her collection of Capri pants, when I stepped on a part of the floor that creaked. Gee, that's strange, a creaky floor in a new condo, I knelt down to take a look.

The closet consisted of hardwood floors, so I pressed again on the floor and noticed that one of the floorboards was loose. I put down the flashlight and knelt down. I ran my hand along the floorboard and felt cold air. I lifted the loose board just a crack, and it slid off, and I shined the light down on it and discovered a small notebook hidden in the floor.
It was a 5x7 diary, and Monet lilies decorated the cover. I scanned a page that said, *"John is finally out of my life, now that he is in prison, I feel so much safer, now I can get on with my life."* I wanted to read

more, but I had the sudden urge that I wasn't going to be alone much longer. I heard a click coming from the front door. I put the loose floorboard back and put the diary in my hoodie pocket.

I slowly crept out of the closet. I made it to the bedroom when I heard the front door close. Frozen like a deer in headlights, I stopped, then thought fast and headed for the bathroom that was just off to the right.

I climbed into the shower stall, shivering with fear. Trying to be as quiet as I could, the dark red shower curtain kept me from being noticed, from God knows who was out there. I searched my hoodie pocket for my small can of pepper spray that I always kept with me. I held it in my hand, I was ready if by some way the intruder pulled back this shower curtain, I would be armed.

I stood motionless and placed my hand over my mouth to keep any noise from coming out, while my other hand held the pepper spray. The intruder was searching the room; there wasn't much to look through, the shower curtain was too close to the door, and I was afraid someone would see me peeking out. I heard papers being shuffled and

plastic covers being moved off the damaged living room furniture. My breathing was shallow, and my brow was starting to sweat. I was mere feet away from the intruder. I knew I had no way out until this person left, and if they were searching for something, what was it that they were looking for?
I heard the footsteps pass the bathroom and head straight for the closet. Hangers and clothes were being thrown off the racks, and the rustling of clothes in dry cleaning bags was tossed to the floor. Then the creaking sound of the floor in the closet, and then the intruder had

found the place where the diary had once been.

I heard a few whispered curses and then a shoe being thrown against the wall. The intruder stalked out of the closet, past the bathroom, and out to the living room. The front door closed with a thud, and the footsteps of the intruder disappeared.

I stepped out of the shower and took a breath of the stale air. I felt sick to my stomach. Ready to puke from the acid creeping up my throat from fear. I had to get out of here and fast before anyone else decided to come marching in.

Deep breaths, Nikki deep breaths, I kept saying to myself. I reached the front door and looked through the peephole. No one was around, and the coast was clear. I opened the door just a crack, looked from side to side, and crept out. I locked the door and put the key under the pot, and went back home. It was 2 am when I got back, and my legs were like jello from the strain of going down the stairs in a panic. I locked my place up tight, checking all my windows and the French doors that led to my patio. I turned out all the lights and ran into my room, locked the door, and hid in bed under the covers.

Still feeling very scared from my near miss, I brought the covers up to my chin. My hand left the safe serenity of my down comforter to find the light switch to my table lamp next to my bed. I had Chanel's diary with me still in my hoodie pocket. I pulled it out and started to read what she said.

December 28,

John and I had dinner in Palm Springs
. Tonight, he was actually in a good mood. Guess
he came into some big money, he gave me a pair

of diamond earrings. Some nice ones. Wonder how long his good behavior will
last. John also mentioned he saw a face from the past,
A guy named Kaid Kendle, whom he used to work for back
in New York. He said that Kaid was part of the
RI Pioneers. A ring of drug kings from New York to
New Jersey, what a crowd he hangs out with.
God, what a loser, what was I thinking?
Break up with him tomorrow.

January 3,
After a night of his abuse, I dumped him and put a restraining order on him. He's not worth the bruises.

Summer went with me to court,
God bless her for all her help.
Got to get life on track, I have an interview next week for a job as an assistant to the mayor,
I need this one.

January 21,

Dear Diary,
He dropped by the apartment and
got physical again. Summer had to call the cops, and now I have a bruise over my eye, and he will spend
six months in the slammer, more if he's on parole.
I guess restraining orders are only good on paper.
But at least it helped in putting him back where he belongs.

Now I have to explain why I have this shiner

to my boss, he's a cool guy, cute but married.

February 28,

Dear diary,

My life is finally getting better.

I have this new job with the city,

a new place to live, and a new love in my

life. It seems like things are looking up.

Grant is fabulous, even though he's the mayor, he's so down to earth

and so funny, good looking, too bad he's married.

March 1,

Dear Diary,

I couldn't help it, but it happened.

As much as I tried to fight the

Urge and how many times I kept reminding myself that he's married,

we did it. Grant and I went to

Santa Maria, in Northern California, for a state conference, and that

night we had dinner, went back to his hotel room, and we made love. It

was beautiful, he's so romantic and caring.

I know I will regret it, but what happens in Santa Maria stays in Santa

Maria.

March 10,

Dear Diary,

We have been very careful not to get caught. Grant and I are still

together. He says that his marriage has been in

Distress for a long time.

He said that getting a divorce would be too Complicated. I don't care as long as I can see him every day.

We are professionals at work;
no one knows or even suspects anything,
but after work, when he has his
city meetings, we leave when all the others leave, and we meet at
Summer's parents' house while they are in Europe for business,
it's just a ten-minute drive from here.

Her journal had me hooked, and on and on I read, going to the kitchen and letting myself relax a bit from my earlier encounter. I put the tea kettle on and made some chamomile. I pulled some scones and a jar of Devonshire from the fridge. I needed a midnight snack to go with my reading. Now here in the kitchen, I had my sweats on and a long-sleeved white T-shirt with pink sleeves. A shirt left over from my time on the pink ladies' baseball team. The tournament from last year's city fundraiser the band played on for charity.
Teacup in hand, I settled on the couch with an afghan.
I read the next couple of pages. From March-May

March 12,

Dear Diary,

I saw Kaid Kendle again. He was at a Chamber of Commerce mixer. He now owns three more restaurants, and no one here in Rancho Niguel. I remember what John said about him being a drug king. Odd that he would own restaurants, but maybe that's his cover. Maybe that's how he doesn't get caught.

March 20

Dear Diary,

Grant said that he loved me...

I can't believe he loves me...

But he's married...

He said he wished he could marry me and have a family with me.
We could go away from here, from his wife and his work, and stop
hiding his feelings for me.
If only we could.

March 25

Dear Diary,

I found a way for us to be together.

It took some heavy thinking, and even though I know I'm playing with
fire, it seems like my only choice.

I met with Kaid Kendle, and I told him that I knew who he was. I told
him that I would carry
that secret to the grave for a small price of $ 2 million dollars. He was
upset, but he agreed to my plan. I'm getting the money tomorrow.

March 26,

Dear Diary,

My plan worked!!

I've never seen so much money in my Life. Kaid kept his promise; he
gave me

a Louis Vuitton tote bag filled with hundreds. Hundreds!!
No one else knows, not even Grant, and now, finally, we have our

chance at happiness. It's a good start for
Grant and me now we can have our dream.

April 4,

Dear diary,
Grant said he needed more time.
I couldn't believe that he was still afraid

to leave her. Why can't he just take a chance? Why can't he see how
much I have done to help us be together?
I told him I would go to
Washington State and buy a home
for us. He told me to take it slow.
He still has a year left of his term in office. He wants to finish it.

April 16,

Dear diary,
After our late-night rendezvous at the office,
I noticed a suspicious car following me. Maybe it's nothing, I know
John is still
in prison, and Kaid said he would never make his presence known to
me.
I feel a little creeped out though!
I hope it's nothing.

April 20

Dear Diary,

Got plastered last night. I had a bad
day with Grant. I keep asking him when we are going to be together.

But he keeps telling me to

be patient.

Is he lying? Stringing me along?

Is he just in it for sex?

It was his wife's birthday today,

and he couldn't see me tonight.

Why doesn't he just leave that wife of his?

I know he hates her, I know she makes him completely miserable.

What about me?

I went to Oliver and Martin's place for drinks, they are a

Girl's best friend.

April 30,

Dear diary,

Today was a bad day.

I was confronted by Grant's wife, who accused me of sleeping with him,

but of course, I denied it. I told her that I respected his work and this

community, and my job.

She told me that if she found out I had

lied, she would make sure I was fired and never work in this town

again.

How did she find out? Were we not careful enough?

May 1,

Dear diary,

I finally put all that money away in a safe place. I felt uneasy about

keeping it here, so I took out a safe deposit box at Rancho Niguel

Credit Union to put all the money in.

For now, it's under Grandma Lilly's name. Coming back from

Summer's place,

that same black car was following me.

May 5,

Cinco de Mayo celebration was a hit at the new cultural center.
We stole a few minutes at the theatre dressing room next to the cultural center.

We kissed, and all of my anxiety was gone. He promised me his marriage was over,
he told me he was tired of his wife, Veronica, and that he would file for a divorce on Monday.

May 8,

Dear diary,
He spoke to his attorney about the divorce. He filed papers, and she will be served
in a few days. Looks like things are changing, and we will be back on track in the future.

May 12,

Dear diary,

I'm so worried now

that John got out of prison. I went to a
Walmart and bought a shotgun. I have to wait on the background check to come back, but I can pick it up soon, hopefully sooner than later.
He will not get in the way of what
Grant and I have. Not this time.

May 15,

Dear diary,

He showed up at the condo. I don't know how

he found out where I live, but he was waiting by the

door, with that smile of his. Like a snake waiting to kill its prey. I dialed

911 as soon as I could and fought with him.

I yelled and screamed, and my neighbors came out and helped me from

being attacked.

Craig, who was home this evening, is a Rancho Niguel cop. He held on

to Amos until the Police, who were close by, got here.

When they took him away, he said

he would find me anywhere; he said he would never let me go.

I was so shaken up, I

stayed with Summer tonight, hope he rots in prison.

May 20,

Dear diary,

Grant took me to the beach. Today we were supposed to be at a

convention in San Diego.

We walked on the beach, and he held me close.

We talked about our plans for the future

playing in the sand and running along the shore.

It was beautiful, collected a few seashells.

Grant knows of an island in Washington State,

A place in the

Sound called Bainbridge Island. It's beautiful, green, and has many

trees all around it with a nice view of the city. To me, it sounds like

freedom.

He took me in his arms and kissed me,

then he bent down on one knee and proposed.

It's a three-karat marquee diamond

set in platinum. I know I have to hide it,

I'll put it in the safe deposit box

until it's safe to have it out.

He said his wife was very upset about the

divorce, and she has contacted her

lawyers. She has gone to Hawaii for

two weeks to take it all in.

I guess she is troubled by

this, even though Grant says they

never loved each other.

He married her

for her political potential.

now it doesn't matter he said he's done with politics he wants to take a

job from a friend of his at The Seattle Times, he said he was a journalist

before he became mayor, he said he never wanted to run for Governor

the way Veronica wanted him too he said she was power hungry for the

white house, he even said that

she has this vision of being the first Lady.

What a character she is; her fantasy is over.

May 26,

Dear diary,

got a strange call, a breather, then a few hang-ups; it really scared

me. Today, Marge from work said that I had a package at my desk from

FedEx. I was excited at first, I thought maybe

it was from Grant, but to my surprise,

it was a dead rat with my name on it. That John Amos, how much lower can he sink?

May 30,

Dear Diary,

This Memorial Day weekend, Grant said
that I should sell the condo and put in my
two-week notice to the city.
He said to start packing small
stuff, and he would hire movers to do the rest.
He said he would drive up to Washington State
with me and then fly back to take care of the
last of his work, which he unofficially
put in for retirement with the city.
I will be putting the condo up for sale; it should sell fast, the area is
new and up and coming, and I will make a good profit from it.
June 3,
Dear diary,
I spoke to a realtor and told her to wait
until I move out to put the condo on the market.

I haven't started packing yet, but I will

get the boxes in a few days. Plus, I will put in my notice to leave my
job.
Grant and Veronica are living in separate
places. She has asked for the house and the car
as far as spousal support.

Grant said Veronica has family money and that she is the
wealthy one; she owes him $6000k a month.

Let's just say that with my two million
and his monthly
income, we will be fine.
We will soon be together forever.

I had spent three hours in Chanel O' Conner's life, and I knew more
than I ever thought I would about her. She wasn't as innocent as we all
thought. Here she was extorting money from Kaid, stealing from a
married man, and blaming her unhappiness on the wife.

It was no wonder Kaid pretended as if he didn't know her. What was he
going to say, oh yeah, she black-mailed me into giving her millions, but
I didn't kill her.
I knew I had to get this over to Detective Anderson so he could make
something of it. Maybe this would be the clue he needed to answer
some of his questions in all of this.

I know it's dangerous to keep it for a while, but how am I going to give
it to him? What do I say? "Oh, not to walk all over your investigation,
but I did illegally acquire this journal of Chanel's by breaking into her
place and searching it until I turned up a clue."

Yeah, he'll be understanding on that one, but Detective Anderson needs
to have it.

He'll be able to put the clues together with what he has, and maybe the real killer will be caught.

I wanted to call someone and tell them what I had learned, but it was too late to call Martin and Oliver. Too late to call Roxy, although she probably is still hanging out right about now. Jessica is probably passed out in her hotel room and won't be nursing her hangover until tomorrow morning.

By 4:30 am, the sun was coming up, and my brain was fried. I turned out the light and went to bed.

CHAPTER 10

Putting It All Together

I woke up early with just four hours of sleep and took a morning jog around the mall.

At 8 am the stores were all closed, but the streets had a few morning walkers. The senior citizen walkers, who usually ended up at the bakery for coffee and pastries, were out this morning. A few new moms pushing strollers and a few daily joggers out for a run. I jogged past Kate's Coffee Hut and inhaled the aroma of fresh Kona coffee, yummmmm.

I made a mental note to grab my coffee after my run. I walked, then jogged, then raced around the corner. I went in the direction of Kendel's Kannery, and lo and behold, parked right in front was Kaid's silver Lamborghini. The front door was unlocked, and from the front window, Kendle spotted me.

He was dressed in Lucky jeans, a white linen shirt, and flip flops. The surfer dude greeted me with his thirty-watt smile,

"Hi, Nikki."

"Hi, Kaid," I said, coming to a stop to greet him.

"So, have you gotten the call for the Mayor's birthday bash?"

"No, not yet, but I'm sure I will soon."

I wanted to ask Kaid if he had any other business dealings in this town, now that I knew how he could afford that race car of his. "Well, let me tell you they are paying very well this year," he said.

"Is that so?" I said, running in place to keep my momentum,

"So good that even the theme is better, it's going to be Mardi Gras." He waved his hands up in the air to show his enthusiasm.

"That should be fun, I know the Mayor loves jazz. Oh, and by the way, did you hear Mayor Mahoney is retiring this year?" I wanted to see his reaction.

"Oh no, I just heard he is going to run for Governor next year."

"You're kidding, Kaid, when did this happen?" I asked and wiped my brow with my towel.

"Last night, he told the city at the open forum and said he would be gearing up for the race, with *the* Mrs. Right by his side."

Running for Governor didn't make any sense, but with Chanel gone, maybe the mayor was going to stay with his wife. Maybe she did have something to do with the murder, maybe fishing for Kaid to be the murderer was leaving me with nothing.

"Kaid, how well do you know Mrs. Mahoney? I mean, what is she like?" I asked.

"Veronica, she's your typical politician's wife, boring, devoted, educated, and very demanding! She comes from a good, wealthy family that kind of stuff, not my type of woman, too high maintenance."

I laughed, "Stefford wife, huh."

He shrugged, "I guess, hey, why all the questions about Mrs. M?"

He lifted his sunglasses to look at me.

"Just curious, that's all, she definitely wears fabulous shoes," I said.

A busboy came outside from the restaurant, calling out.

"Kaid, your shipment of lobster is here."

"My lobster, oh yes, for the party, I got to get back to work, talk to you later," he waved.

"Bye," I waved back.

The busboy gave a strong, hard stare. I began to wonder if he had done any time. His dark eyes were deep and his jaw tight, and his torso strong. A tattoo of a gang symbol was on his hand.

I could barely make out 42nd St. In small green lettering. No doubt a gang from LA, what kind of people did Kaid employ?

I ran back around the mall one last time and then went for the Kona blend. I sat in the sun to soak up some rays, my sunblock of SPF 35 working hard against the morning sun.

The busboy at Kendel's had me wondering if Kaid had a new network here, selling drugs.

I didn't want to believe he was behind any of this. He was a great guy, not my type, but I had considered dating him when we met. I had been off again at the time with Matt, but for some reason, our timing was never right, so we never went out. Then, when the band was hired by him to play at the restaurant, I kept it professional, and so did he.

Later that day, I got the call for Little Black Dress to play at the mayor's birthday bash at the Cultural Arts Center.
A good gig for us, we were looking at a cha-ching $7k gig for one night.
To a theme of Mardi Gras, as Kaid had mentioned, there would be costumes and jazz and plenty of gumbo provided by Kendle's Kannery.
I showered up and put on my denim capris and a fitted white t-shirt, and a pair of red mules.

I let my long dark hair down today, but put on a thin red headband. I put in a call to Roxy to give her the news.
"Roxy here." She always answered her phone that way.
"Hey, Roxy, what are you doing for lunch today?"

Two things bothered me

1. How was I going to give the journal to Detective Anderson (Paul)?

2. Someone was looking for this, and I needed to find out who.

I walked into Sprouts Market to get a few things for lunch. After talking to Roxy about lunch plans, I realized that the only thing in my fridge was a bowl of fresh veggies and a six-pack of Pierre. I had a list of items: Cesar salad, chicken, wine, ice cream for dessert, milk, strawberries, Rainer cherries, the usual stuff.
Sprouts had its usual rush, the deli was full, and so I went to get the

fruit. My mind was still going a million miles, so I walked through the store on autopilot.

"It seems like we keep running into each other?"

I turned around and met Matt's gaze.

"You're here again, Matt."

"Just getting dinner for the guys at the station, it's my turn to cook." He was in his navy pants and a short-sleeved shirt. He always looked so cute in that uniform, standing here in the produce section.

"That's sweet, Matt, so tell me, do you still make a great meatloaf and mashed potatoes?" I asked while picking up some bags of cherries.

"Number 1 second year in a row."

He said, boasting and tossing oranges in his basket.

"So, why do I always see you here? Shouldn't you be with Summer, what's her name?"

"She's working tonight," he smiled.

"Oh, too bad," I replied with sincerity, walking past him.

"Nikki, can I be honest with you?"

I turned around and gave him my full attention.

"Yes," I said, wondering why he was getting so serious now.

"I know that you still care about me, but you broke up with me, and if that's the way you wanted it, then you should let me move on."

He said.

Stunned and knowing fully that this wasn't a joke, I said,

"Excuse me, Matt, what are you talking about?"

"Nikki, I know about the phone calls," he said, looking disappointed.

"What phone calls, Matt?" I said, looking very puzzled, standing in the produce section holding a container of organic blueberries.

He chuckled. "What phone calls, you know the ones you've been making to Summer, telling her to stay away from me, calling late at night and hanging up."

Now I was wondering if he was smoking something!

"What! I didn't make any phone calls to her. Are you crazy? I don't even have her number. Look, Matt, yeah, I still care about you, but I'm not a fatal attraction, ok, you can date anyone you like, but don't come around telling me I'm harassing your girlfriend when I'm not. You know me better than that."

He put his hands on his hips and looked up at the ceiling as if he was trying to take it all in, then he rolled his eyes, ran his hand over the top of his hair, and exhaled

"Look, just stop harassing her!"

I looked him straight in the eyes and said in a calm, cool manner,

"I don't care what you do, Matt, and by the way, I'm seeing someone myself, all right, I have moved on, so tell Polly Anna to stop lying." His face was very serious now.

"You're seeing someone, who is he?"

"He happens to be a cop. Detective Anderson, I'm sure you know who he is."

"Yeah, I know him."

"Well then, there you go, I'm not stocking your girlfriend."

He was quiet for a moment, just standing there looking at me.

"I need to get going, I have to get this food for the guys at the station."

"I have a lot to do today, too," I said, anger burning in my throat and hurt in my eyes.

He turned to leave, then turned around toward me again. He put down the small grocery basket and came close to me. He held my hands.

"Nikki, I want you to be happy, that's all I ever wanted for you, and if it's with Anderson or anyone else, I just want you to be happy."

"Thank you, Matt, I hope you're happy too."

It was an awkward moment, having him hold my hands and feeling the warmth of his touch, in the produce department, yet it was something I missed so much.

Looking into his eyes, I felt myself pouring my heart out to him, but with no words.

He got a call on his radio,

"This is Lt. Stevens." He took the call and confirmed his location.

"I have to go, we got an industrial fire on Rochester Lane," he kissed me on the cheek, went to pay for his groceries, and headed out to the parking lot, where a large white fire truck picked him up.

I met Roxy for lunch at 1:00 pm, and we decided to go out instead of my place for lunch. She had a class at 11 in the morning that she taught at the Community Center twice a week called Drumming For Your Soul.

Roxy's version of teaching many techniques for the perfect jamming session with your friends.

She is extremely proud of it, and her classes are always full all the time, and she even has a waiting list.

With a pair of black jeans and a black halter top, she sat down and put her drumsticks on the table.

"Do you ever go anywhere without those things, Roxy?" I asked her,

"They go where I go," she said, picking up the menu and scanning it with her heavy mascara-laden fake eyelashes.

"So what color do you have on today?" I asked.

Roxy has the biggest collection of red lipsticks I have ever seen; it's the only color she puts on her full collagen-loaded lips. Her vanity at her place has two drawers full of every red ever made in lipstick. "You like, it's called Very Scary Red Slasher. It's from the vampire line."

"It's cool, I like it! Anyway, I have to tell you what's going on."

We spent the next 45 minutes eating Angel hair pasta, and I went into detail about everything that I had found out from the diary. Plus, the incident with Matt and the harassment he accused me of.

"Wow, talk about some crazy stuff," she said, finishing her cranberry juice.

"So what are you going to do about the book? You have to turn that over to the police. This really changes everything. What if Kaid did the killings? I mean, 42nd street man was probably the one who did the hit for Kaid. You said he was a badass-looking kind of guy, right?"

"Yeah, I think he is a good suspect, after all, Kaid had all the motive in the world."

"No kidding! So how was the date with Mr. Hottie with the handcuffs?" Only Roxy could put it that way as she changed the subject from murder to romance.

"It was good, he's a nice guy."

"But you're still in love with Mr. Firehose, that it?"

"Trust me, the last thing I need now is a love triangle. Matt seems pretty comfortable with his sweet little Polly Anna, the perfect." I used my hands to show my quotations for the nickname I gave her.

"I can't believe he accused you of making phone calls to harass her, that's not like you, it's like me, but not you. Matt knows that he's got his head up his ass, don't worry, he'll come around."

We ordered chocolate cake for dessert and made a list of what I had so far. We went over it forwards and backward, and still, neither one of us came up with anything new, so we gave it a rest for now.

"Gotta go, Nancy Drew, keep me informed, and if you want to snoop, give me a call. It sounds like a blast." I kissed her on the cheek and gave her a hug.

"Ok, I'll call you later."

4:00 pm rolled around, and I needed some caffeine, so I called Oliver and Martin. I needed to bring them up to speed, too!

"Hey, guys, meet me at Starbucks in the mall. I have to tell you what happened.

"Okay, Nikki, but it better be good. Martin is in the middle of selling the Staccato painting overseas. We're almost done, give us 15, okay."

"Sure, I'll see you then."

I put on a light jacket and then walked over to the mall.

The Starbucks at the outdoor mall was much larger than the one where Jessica worked. There was an outdoor patio with green umbrellas and teak tables, and chairs. I picked a spot under the white trellis with ivy and roses on the top and the sides of the patio. It was a warm evening, and the Santa Ana winds were casually breezing by.

My cell rang with the melody of jazz music from Wynton Marsalis playing a soft tune.

"Hello."

"Stay away from Matt, if you know what's good for you." The line went dead, and it left me freaked out. I looked at the number on the screen of my cell phone, and it said *PUBLIC.*

That meant that someone obviously used a pay phone, and since there were very few of them left, that meant either a city or county building, an airport, or a hotel.

A sharp chill ran down my spine. What the heck was that about?

Then I thought maybe it was Summer. After what Matt told me earlier today about harassing her with phone calls. She was so pissed the other night at Kiana's party, she gave me the evil eye the whole night.

Obviously, she thinks I'm still after Matt, which made the most sense in my mind, so she's blowing off steam and getting back at me.

"Hey, honey, what's up?" Oliver asked, coming up behind me. "You look like you've seen a ghost!" Martin said,

"Oh, I just got this weird phone call, it freaked me out, but I don't think it's anything to worry about."

"Do tell," Oliver said, taking a seat next to me.

"Oh, it's nothing, just Matt's girlfriend is playing a prank on me, she called and said to stay away from Matt if you know what's good for you." "Honey, that's serious! The back off, my man attitude is a total Play Misty for me moment. You'd better be careful."
Oliver replied.

"Oliver, they haven't even been together that long, two months maybe three. Don't you think that's a little strange to be so possessive?" I remarked,

"Nikki, have you seen Play Misty for me? You know Clint Eastwood at his babe moment and the lovely Donna Mills." Martin asked,

"Oh, she's always fabulous, Martin." Oliver said

"I agree but I've never seen it," I said

"Oh Martin let me tell the story, okay well here it goes, it takes place in beautiful Carmel California, by the ocean and it has a great musical score, jazz, old-time jazz anyway Clint was with Donna and they were like in love and then he wanted to play the field you know got scared of commitment that kind of thing, anyway they break up, Donna goes away out of town for a while and Clint baby plays the field, he meets Evelyn played by, oh Martin what's her name it escapes me?

"Jessica Walter," Martin says,

"Yes, that's right, Jessica Walter, she's fabulous. Anyway, he meets her, and she looks hot to him, so he takes her back to his place, they make beautiful love and have this magical connection, and all is well. Then the next day, when Clint is over the "magic."

Oliver used his fingers to make quotations.

"She keeps coming back for seconds, and he starts getting a little tired of her, but he doesn't stop sleeping with her. They have maybe three or four flings, and he gets tired of her coming around. She's making him breakfast, she gets a key to his place from his landlord, she gets really possessive, and she's got a bad temper on her. Anyway, he tells her to get lost. Then he finds out that Donna is back in town, so he's ready to go back to his old girlfriend, but Evelyn can't take it; she's got them walking down the aisle and everything.

She even follows Clint around and finds him making out with Donna on the beach. So to make a long story short she starts acting out violently she tries to kill his housekeeper, she follows him around and starts destructing his career, then she goes after Donna, that's where it gets really sick, and then at the end, Clint throws her over a cliff, but believe me no one can play psycho like a jilted or over possessive anything."

"You think Summer is Evelyn and I'm Donna and Matt is Clint, wow, I'm going to have to see that movie."

"Oh yeah, the seventies fashions are back in too, but keep in mind there are a lot of Evelyns out there, be on your guard, I wouldn't take this too lightly if I were you, and tell Matt, he needs to know this, maybe he can talk some sense into her."

113

Martin and Oliver looked worried, and they even suggested I get some extra pepper spray just in case.

"Well, guys, that's not why I called you two over here. I didn't want to tell you over the phone, but here goes:"

I told them how and where I found the journal and about my moment of suspense with the intruder with no face. They had looks of complete shock!

Martin spoke up first.

"I know Veronica Mahoney is responsible, and the journal proves it. She did know what was going on, and I think she was the one following Chanel." He looked deep in thought, thinking very carefully over what he was saying.

"What about Kaid, what if he was the one following Chanel, maybe he was trying to get his $2 million back, maybe he had John Amos killed, I heard him on the phone talking about not making any more mistakes what if he sent someone to kill John and take the fall for him killing Chanel," I commented, they took in my theory and looked to be measuring what we now know to what the facts were so far.

Martin spoke first, holding his finger up in an I have an idea way, his eyes fixed on ours, he whispered.

"What if he is in on this thing with Veronica? What if the two of them conspired to kill Chanel?" Oliver and I sat back and thought about this. It made sense, but there was still one fact.

"But how would she know that Kaid had been blackmailed by Chanel?"

We all sat in silence for a moment to take it all in.

The blackmail, the murder, the affair, the stalking, the lie.

Who would have thought all of this was going on in this nice, warm, sunny Southern California city?

The Santa Ana breeze came with new energy, and the Ficus trees and small fan palms whistled with a high-pitched cry. My bare arms chilled with goosebumps from the wind.

"We need to find out who Veronica Mahoney is," I said, breaking the thick wall of silence.
They looked at me in unison and nodded their heads.
"How can we help?"

CHAPTER 11

Date Number 2

I had invited Paul over for dinner this evening, it seemed like the last date we had ended with his murder suspect committing suicide. When I called him earlier today, he was in better spirits. He picked up right away on the first ring,

"Hi, I'm glad you called. Of course, I would love to come over for dinner. Is 7 pm ok?"

He asked.

"Seven it is, bring your appetite."

"Ok, I will, see ya then."

I put on Miles Davis on my iPhone and connected it to my small pocket speaker. I opened a bottle of Chardonnay and poured myself a glass; the delicate aroma of floral and peach scents filled the air.

It was nearly seven, and my dinner of Chicken Piccata with angel hair pasta was done. I placed the food on my new Tuscan serving dishes that I had bought at William Sonoma; they always have great stuff there. I garnished it with parsley, and boom, it was ready. I set the table with a white linen tablecloth and yellow cloth napkins.

The garden salad with tomatoes, cucumber slices, and shredded Romano cheese made my mouth water.

The doorbell rang at 7 pm sharp. Goodman, punctual.

He looked incredible, grey button-down shirt and a pair of black pants, he looked right out of GQ magazine.

"Hi, these are for you." His eyes sparkled, handing me a bouquet of red roses.

"Thank you, they're beautiful."

I put the roses in a vase and placed them on the table.

"You have Miles on, I like it, you have great taste."

"Of course, I have a Jazz station on Pandora, it shuffles with a selection of Diana Krall and Ella Fitzgerald, new Jazz, Old Jazz, I love it all.

He sat down, and I handed him a glass of wine.

"Can I help with anything?"

"No, it's all done."

I brought two dinner plates and set them down, along with the salad dishes. I collected my wine glass from the breakfast bar and sat across from him at the table.

"Thank you, I'm not used to being so pampered." He smiled,

"Well, you are the guest, and I am an incredible host. I love doing this kind of stuff, dinner parties, cooking."

"A person could get used to this."

I smiled with confidence at one of my three talents.

He took a bite of his chicken and then grabbed my hand.

"This is amazing, this is restaurant quality."

"I'm glad you like it."

"Like it! Can I have you make dinner for me every night?"

I laughed a bit.

"So, it's true then?"

He placed his napkin on his lap. "What is?"

"The way to a man's heart is through his stomach." I patted my tummy, mocking the old cliche.

"Yes, I would marry you." Flashing that wonderful smile of his,

I chucked. "We are on our second date."

He smiled.

"You mean we're not on our third date yet." He replied in reference to his previous statement of dates that were walking him down the aisle on date three.

"Not yet!" I smiled and decided to switch gears to the case.

"So how are things at work?"

"Work is busy."

I sensed that maybe he didn't want to talk shop tonight, so I let it go.

Our conversation flowed lightly and naturally, discussing normal things. I told him about the new dress I bought at Anne Taylor, and the new fountain the city is putting in at the library, the fabulous paintings at Martin and Oliver's gallery.

Pretty much everything except the murder and the journal.

"Would you like to go surfing with me sometime?"

"Wow! Me surf?" I finished the last of my wine and carefully pondered getting in the water and attempting to surf. I have to admit I was a little scared of the thought of it.

"I've been surfing since I was ten, and I'm really big on safety, so you can trust me."

He looked so excited at the prospect of teaching me how to surf. I gave in and said,

"I'd love for you to teach me how to surf. It would be fun to learn something new and adventurous."

"Are you a good swimmer?"

"Two years of Varsity swim in college," I replied.

He pointed to himself and said,

"Four years in college, fastest backstroke on my team." He beamed.

I was happy at what we had in common; it gave us one more thing to talk about. He was easy to be with. Comfortable, and he put me at ease. I felt like we had always been friends.

"So where did you go to college?" I asked,

"USC, I'm a Trojan." He proudly stated, referring to the University of Southern California. (University of Spoiled Children is usually what goes through my mind)

"Let me guess a degree in History." I asked,

"No more like Psychology."

"Uh oh, are you analyzing me?" I teased

"You have nothing to worry about. What about you, school?"

"I went to USD (University of San Diego), I'm a Torero, that's our mascot, a bullfighter. I was pre-law."

"The University of San Diego, and pre-law, a Catholic girl?"

"Yes, my parents wanted me to go there. I did love it, I'm not going to lie, it was a great school, and I earned a degree in Sociology with a crime, justice, and law concentration."

"Really."

I knew he was wondering why I'm singing my heart out as a restaurant entertainer instead of working as a lawyer for some fancy law firm.

"I know what you're thinking, why am I not a Lawyer?"

"I am curious, what made you change direction?"

"Well, I had graduated from USD, and I was going to go to graduate school there the following Fall semester, but my parents had a very messy divorce, and when they split, my mom stayed here in California, and my Dad moved to Florida, with his secretary.

A few months later, he and his new wife were killed in a plane crash off Key West.

My mom took it pretty hard. She was still in love with him, and she had a bit of an emotional setback. So I took some time off to help her, and we went to grief counseling and helped each other with our loss.

She and I moved to San Francisco a few years after that; she wanted to get away for a while. I worked as a paralegal in a law office there in Frisco, and that's when my mom met Jeff. A multi-billionaire in the software industry, they fell in love and got married a year later.

Now my mom has a busy life with running charities and having parties to raise money for a lot of different causes. She is very happy, and Jeff is a great man, so I have no complaints. So knowing she was secure, I came back home to Rancho Niguel, and I got a place to live with Roxy, who went to USD with me. So one night we went to this club in

Hollywood, and she knew the owner, so we got in with no cover charge, and he had his band cancel on him.

He was really in a bind because they were having some special dedication that night, and they hired a live band to give it more energy. So, Roxy, being the crazy and wild spirit that she is, told the owner we would sing and be his entertainment.

She called a few girls we went to high school with, and they came by, and we just played our hearts out. In high school, it was just for fun, but this was a paying gig, and we had some amazing feedback that evening, so we gave ourselves a name and became a band. I love singing; it just makes me feel strong and confident. It's not like having a real musical career, and I'm fine with that. I'm not looking for fame.

All the girls have full-time jobs, and none of them are married. This is a part-time hobby for them. Roxy has a biology degree and works as a lab tech for a research company. As for me, I just never had the urge to go back to school for that law degree.

Jeff, my stepdad, suggested I invest in a start-up computer company that a friend of his was putting together. I had a little cash from my dad's estate, and it came through. It gave me an awesome return, and so I bought this condo, and I invest in a few things here and there, and I just built up my portfolio, so I am pretty well set, and I'm happy."

"That's quite a story." He looked blown away. Maybe I gave him too much info too fast.

"I'm sorry, I guess I just got carried away. I don't know why I told you all this. Remember, we're just on our second date." I smiled

"I'm glad you told me. I admire you, you're a strong, independent woman. You have your own money and home, no one tells you when to work, I'm inspired. I'm also sorry for your loss, about your dad."
"Thank you." I smiled.
After dinner, he helped me clear the dishes and put them in the dishwasher, we laughed about the last episode of The Big Bang Theory, and we talked about who would go to the World Series this year. The Dodgers, Yay.

I felt like I was already in a relationship with Paul; we have chemistry, and he is also a major hottie.
When we were done in the kitchen, we went out to the patio, and I switched the music to Chris Botti. I turned out the lights inside and lit some candles. Recently, I purchased some outdoor lantern lighting for summer evenings like these.

My patio set consisted of a small loveseat and two chairs, made of sea grass, which is like a woven kind of grass. It's very comfy with soft cushions in a yellow garden print. I have to say I have fallen asleep in them a time or two.

The patio was now dim and sparkling with my new lights. We sat and enjoyed our dessert of a cup of white tea and a slice of tiramisu cake.
"This tea is good, usually, I'm a coffee drinker, but I think I've been consuming too much caffeine?"

"White tea is my favorite tea; it has a light flavor to it, and I buy it from a tea house that carries tea from all over the world."

I opened the lid of my Russian Lomonosov teapot to show him the large green leaves.

"Whole, tea, wow, are you a connoisseur?"

"Kind of, just to let you know the stuff in bags doesn't do it for me, it's chopped up, and that basically ruins tea."

"Good to know."

"Oh, I'm not a tea snob or anything."

He just chuckled.

We made small talk during dessert, and the whole time I kept thinking, I really like this guy. For the moment, I felt that I could see Paul and I had a future together.

Our empty dessert plates were on the table. Paul took charge and carried the dishes inside, and washed them. 20 points for doing dishes, yes! He came back out after he put the dishes away for me, and he brought my Ivory afghan.

"I thought you might need this."

He draped it over me

"Thanks."

He sat back down next to me on the loveseat and started rubbing my back.

"Can you come over and wash dishes and give me a massage every day, too?"

His hands were warm and gentle but firm.

As he rubbed out the knots, I closed my eyes and just enjoyed my massage.

"I might be able to work at least two nights a week for you."

When he was finished, I turned to him and looked into his eyes. He cupped my face with his hands and kissed me.

His lips were warm and soft. I closed my eyes and returned his kiss. With the soft lighting and music, we kissed a little more, and then we put the brakes on. I wanted to move very slowly.

We sipped our tea, and I rested my head on his shoulder. His warm breath was just above my forehead; it was calming and smooth.

His voice trailed slowly as he was talking about the new surfboard that he bought. Then we both fell fast asleep on the patio, with the moonlight as our blanket and the stars as our nightlight.

Chapter 12

Meeting Mrs. M

I woke up early with a new burst of energy. After a shower, I made some Kona coffee in the French press, which I might add is the best way to enjoy a fantastic cup of coffee. I toasted a bagel, added a heap of cream cheese, and voila, breakfast of champions. Paul was still asleep on the patio sofa, and he looked so peaceful, so I covered him with the Ivory afghan. I didn't want to wake him up.

I put my long dark hair in a blue Dodgers cap. Zipped up my dark blue jeans and put on a white short-sleeve fitted polo shirt.

A little mascara, eyebrows, foundation, and of course a flesh color lipstick, never leave the house without makeup, not that I'm obsessive with vanity, but I like having a fresh face of color.

Okay, I admit Sundays are make-up-free unless I have a date, which is rare.

Veronica Mahoney was first on my list for things to do today, but what should I say? I can't just go up to her and accuse her of murdering her husband's mistress. I had to find out where she was the night of the murder, and I had to see if she knew anything about the relationship. Obviously, she had confronted Chanel and asked her if she was having

an affair with her husband. I knew that because it was in the journal.
My cell chimed away, I looked at the caller ID, and it said PUBLIC

On the screen in block letters. I hesitated for a moment. What
if it were my friendly little stalker, Summer? Is she calling me early in
the morning just like a tormented teen? Maybe it's time to face her and
just tell her that her childish tactics were downright stupid.

I answered with a stern "Hello."

There was a brief silence, and right away I thought maybe I would start
to hear heavy breathing right about now.

"Nikki, is that you!"

It was Mrs. Green, and she sounded tired!

"Yes, Mrs. Green, you sound a little tired. Are you ok?" I asked her,

"I'm so sorry I'm calling you so early, but I worked to cover a shift last
night at the hospital. I was wondering if you could do me a big favor
because I can't get home till about noon."

"Sure, Mrs. Green, what do you need?"

"Well, I forgot I'm having a new couch dropped off at 9 am.
Can you let the furniture delivery men in? My spare key is in the large
planter beside the door."

"Absolutely, Mrs. Green, no problem."

"Thanks, Nikki. I owe you one, and I apologize for the early call."

"It's ok, I'm glad to help."

"Thank you so much, bye."

I heard the shower running, and so I made another bagel for Paul and
set out some fresh cantaloupe to go with it.

"Good morning," he said, coming to the table 15 minutes later.

"Good morning, sorry I don't sleep in very much," I said, handing him some coffee.

"Thanks, I don't usually sleep in either," he smiled. "The patio sofa was extremely comfortable."

"It's not the first time I've fallen asleep outside. I get so busy, and it's like a small oasis for me, my own little getaway."

"Sure, I can see that, hey, I'm sorry to eat and run, but I have an early meeting." He said, looking a little sad to be cutting out so soon.
"No problem, I have a big day too."
He slipped on his shoes by the door. "Can I see you later?"

"Yes, I'll call you."
We said goodbye with a kiss, a long one.

I finished up breakfast, put on my new white canvas Keds, and headed out to Mrs. Green's condo to receive her couch.
By the time the furniture delivery guys left, it was 9:45 am, and I had two hang-ups. I put the key back where I found it and made my way out to the bug.

Top-down, black Kate Spade shades on, and I was rolling. My second set of business of the day was to speak with Veronica Mahoney.
I walked into the new City Hall lobby, the sun shone in through the large floor-to-ceiling glass windows. The smell of fresh paint and plaster, with a hint of citrus, greeted me. I walked up to the reception

desk, where a woman in her twenties was busy answering a multi-line black phone.

I waited patiently while she spoke to someone.

Tick tock, tick tock ... . . .

"Oh, yes, please come in and fill out an application. The second floor is human resources, and you want to speak with Cindy, she's the director, and she'll be able to give you details on the interview process, yes, okay, thank you, and have a great day."

She pulled the headset off and turned to me, her bright green eyes shining with enthusiasm. "How can I help you today?"

"Hi, I'm Nikki Rodriguez. I'm with the band Little Black Dress, we are going to play at the mayor's birthday bash, and I was wondering if I could have a word with Mrs. Veronica Mahoney. I just had some questions about setting up and the times of arrival."

"Oh, absolutely, but Mrs. Mahoney isn't here today, but I will tell you this, the venue for the party has been changed, it's going to be held at the Mayor's home instead," she said, smiling brightly.

"Well, yes, I would need that information; it would be crucial," I replied.

"You know, let me call over to Marge, she's the Mayor's assistant, and she could probably give you more info than I can, hold on one second," she said, holding up her index finger to indicate one moment.

"Hi Marge, do you think you could come down here and talk to Miss Nikki Rodriguez? She's with one of the bands for the Mayor's party, uh huh, yes, I told her the location has been changed, okay, I'll send her right up, thanks, Marge."

She hung up the phone and said, "You can go right upstairs, it's the fourth door on the left."

"Thank you."

I headed up a large rod iron staircase, the white adobe walls were smooth and clean, and the mahogany wood on the stairwell gleamed brightly.

At the top of the stairs, the Mahogany floor continued throughout the second floor like a river of wood.

I reached the fourth door, an all-glass door, one with the name in black letters read, MAYOR GRANT MAHONEY.

I saw Marge at her desk, and when she saw me, she smiled.

"Hi, Marge, how are you?" I asked when I entered the office.

"Oh, hello dear, I remember you from Kiana's candle party." She was in a black skirt and a white eyelet blouse that flowed lightly and briskly with her movements.

"That's right, I live in the same building as her."

"Yes, dear, I didn't know your band was Little Black Dress, how marvelous. Now let me see, I need to get you the information pack that we are giving out to everyone that's a part of this shin ding," she said, pushing her glasses up closer to her eyes and heading to a large espresso-colored wooden file cabinet.

The décor was beautiful. The room was a dark sage color with dark

espresso furniture, desks, and file cabinets. The crown molding was white and ran on the top and the bottom of the large two-room office.

The hardwood floors smelled of lemon polish and looked to be golden oak.

"Here they are," she brought out a white folder with the city emblem on the front.

"This is for you, dear; all of the information should be in there."

"Thank you, Marge, that's great, but hey listen do you think it would be possible to speak with Mrs. Mahoney about going out to her home so I can see the layout for the stage, it's something I always do for my clients so I can better serve them," I said hoping this would get me in to see Veronica.

"Well," she thought for a moment,

"Let me give her a ring."

She went to her neat and tidy desk and flipped through her Rolodex, pulled out a card, and dialed Mrs. Mahoney's home number.

"Hello, Mrs. Mahoney, sorry to disturb you, madam, but I have one of the band members here from Little Black Dress, and she would like to know if she could see the layout of the property to prepare for the Mayor's birthday party."

I could see through the glass door to the Mayor's private office; the lights were out, and the desk was bare of any papers, only a desk lamp, a black telephone, and some silver picture frames.

"Oh, thank you, Mrs. Mahoney, I know she will appreciate that, thank you, dear, bye-bye."

"Well, I have good news, Mrs. Mahoney said you can come by right now; she is home for the next few hours, with the party committee. So this is the perfect time for you. Here's the address."

She handed me a piece of paper with the directions.

"It's really easy to find, just take Palm Canyon Rd. all the way up the hill and then take a right on Clark Gable Dr. and then make a left on Morning Hill Way.

You'll end up on a private road called Desert Rose Lane, take that all the way to the private gate and ring the bell at the entrance."

"Thank you, Marge, this really helps, you don't know how much."

"You're welcome, dear, take care."

Out to the bug I went and drove to find more info on this case.

The directions Marge gave me were perfect. I got to the gate and pushed the red button on the black box that stood to the side of the car. There was a loud buzz, and then a voice came from the box,

"Mahoney Residence, may I help you?"

"Hi, my name is Nikki Rodriguez with the band Little Black Dress."

"Hello, Ms. Rodriguez, we've been expecting you."

The tall iron gates parted, and I was allowed passage to the estate. It all seemed so grand, like a commercial for fine fragrances or Ralph Lauren clothes. Old Money and very traditional.

I drove in and followed a long driveway through two rows of palm trees. I came to the Mediterranean villa before me, man, was it a crib and a half! You could've parked a fleet of BMWs in this lot; it was so large.

The house was on a hill, with a circular drive and surrounded by flower beds and a bright green lawn. I walked up the four steps to the front doors.

Frosted tall glass doors with palm trees etched on them.

I rang the doorbell, and through the doors, I could see a woman with her hair in a tight bun, and a knee-length black dress with a lace French apron on.

"Good day, Ms. Rodriguez, please come in."

The ivory marble floors shone so brightly you could slip and slide on them cool I wonder if you could mattress surf on the staircase.

I was led past the formal living room that was decorated in all white and a dining room with the same color scheme. The only color came from the Georgia O' Keefe paintings of flowers that filled the pale walls. It seemed a little lonely or boring with everything being white.

We went past the white gourmet kitchen with copper pans, a copper fridge, and appliances that cost more than my two-bedroom condo.

Finally, we reached a set of French doors that opened to a huge patio. It was about as big as the pool and patio at my condo complex, Olympic-sized, clearly.

The pool gleamed with sparkly reflections from the sun and reflected dancing waves against the patio floor. There were two large groups of people, some had on uniforms from a party rental company, two men in suits holding clipboards, and a man with a bouquet of different flowers wearing a bright yellow blazer and black slacks stood next to two women in sundresses.

My guess was that the help for the party was all here.

I searched for the Mrs. but I couldn't find her; the only one in charge seemed to be a blond older woman with a tight French twist and dressed in a lavender pantsuit.

"All right now, everyone, please follow me, and I will show you where to check in on the night of the party. You all will require a photo ID badge. Security will be tight, so no badge, no enter, get it, people!"

The group of people nodded, and so did I. The housekeeper had left my side and gone off to the house. I walked over to the group and mixed in. Refreshments were brought out on a large ceramic patio table: tall chilled glasses of pink lemonade and red fruit punch, and bottled water for us to enjoy.

I took a glass of fruit punch and sipped away. Behind me, two girls in sun dresses were speaking in soft tones.

"Did you see the order she faxed me? The cake of that size might topple, I told her we could make some adjustments, but she refused to hear it, she said either give me what I need or I'll find someone else to do it!"

"No! Are you serious? I was under the impression that she was the civilized one."

"Oh no, it's either her way or the highway, trust me, she definitely has claws under those fancy gloves she wears."

I had only seen Mrs. Mahoney from afar. I knew she was well educated and that her family was wealthy; now I knew my instincts were right on about her personality.

"Well , hello, everyone."

All the party vendors and I turned away from the refreshment table to face none other than Mrs. Mahoney.

"I hope you all are enjoying those icy drinks, with it being such a scorcher today, I thought it would be a good idea.

Now I have had Tina" (lavender suit lady I assumed) "give you a brief introduction in regards to where you will enter and the id badge that will be very important, I'm going to send you all home with a kit that consists of passes that have your name and the name of the company you work for, now understand we need the pictures of all the employees you wish to bring with you that day.

We require a color copy of your California driver's license or state ID. Each pass has a barcode on it, and once you send us back the photos and passes filled with your information, my security will put them in the computer and give them right back to you. Now it's very important that you have them ready by tomorrow at 10 am. My security will pick them up and then drop off the laminated passes to you by 5 pm. On the day of the event, you will enter through the gate by giving the guard your ID badge, it will be scanned by the barcode, and then you will be able to enter."

She stood ramrod straight, just like a strict school teacher waiting patiently for her students to comprehend the assignment.

The stylish brown medium-length hairdo she had went lovely with her very expensive yellow A-line sleeveless dress.

Her white leather pumps were classic Chanel.

She looked very elegant and very fashionable, what am I saying, she could be a possible murderer.

"Now, are there any questions? If not, we will proceed on the tour." No one said a word, so she proceeded.

"Fine then, let us start with party rentals. You'll be setting up this area of the lawn for the reception tables. Now, I'd like the buffet table set on serpentine tables. I like the look of the buffet curving like a snake; it gives it an interesting angle.

Next, I need round 80-inch tables, and I want gold chairs with padded seats. Next, I'd like about 15" highball tables scattered in the bar area. For the linens, I need metallic gold, fuchsia, bright green, aqua blue, Purple, and bright orange. After all, this is Mardi Gras theme, right?"

Everyone nodded in acceptance.

The party people were busily jotting down all of Mrs. Mahoney's wishes like elves working on Santa's Christmas list.

"I need the stage, lighting over here on the other side of the pool, and give me some of those stage curtains in metallic fuchsia, next I need my balloon people, you'll be dressed in costumes I assume and I'll need you to be making balloons in the shapes of two Mardi Gras masks, those will be put out front and then I need a few bunches of balloons with very long strings to float all around the property, make sure you weight them down so they look like they are ready for takeoff. She was going a million miles a minute. What was she on?

This went on for another hour, she rattled off about water mermaids in the pool, the baker with a cake to resemble the famous Bourbon Street, an Eiffel Tower cake, and a cake of everything New Orleans, bright and colorful. Now I knew why the bakery girls were stressed.

By the time she got to the bands, I was on my third fruit punch and in great need of a bathroom, pronto.

"Hello, Ms. Rodriguez," Mrs. Mahoney said, shaking my hand.

"Hello, it's nice to officially meet you," I replied.

"Let me just say that I enjoy your singing, and I knew that evening at Kendle's when you sang "Someone to Watch Over Me," it was breathtaking. I knew your band would be perfect for this evening."

"Thank you, we are very honored to be participating in this event."

"Well, I think your music will add to the style of the evening, it'll be fabulous."

"Yes, I'm sure it will be. Did you have any special songs in mind, any requests?"

She paused for a moment. "Well, let me think, just keep it slow, sultry kind of jazz, I have two bands from New Orleans coming to play Dixie land jazz, New Orleans Jazz, and of course, your band.

I tried to get the Neville Brothers, but they have a concert in Florida, so this is it."

"I'm sure it will be amazing, Mrs. Mahoney."

"Thank you, it will be, after all, we will also be announcing Mr. Mahoney's candidacy for Governor. It has to be perfect."

"Wow, Governor!" I acted surprised.

"Oh yes, Mr. Mahoney is very excited and pleased to have all the supporters he has garnered through the Mayor's position, but as I always say, move forward, first the mayor's office, then the Governor's office, then of course the White House."

She smiled with confidence as though it was all planned and ready to go.

She really was pining for First Lady; she had a lust for power, and possibly murder.

"This really comes as a shock. I was told that Mr. Mahoney would be retiring."

I said. I chose my words carefully, all the while studying her face to see if she would give any telltale signs to my invasive question.

"Oh no, those were hideous rumors that were started by less-than-friendly reporters in this area."

She said with a stern look upon her face.

Then her happy Stepford-wife look returned to her plastic, airbrushed face.

"Oh, but don't worry, I've taken care of that, so I know I can count on your support for us in the Governor's race."

One thought came to my mind when I was little: my grandmother always said If you know someone is crazy, don't argue with them, just smile and agree with them until you are safely away from them.

After all, this was her home, her domain, so I took Grandma's advice.

"Oh, absolutely, Mrs. Mahoney."

She let out a deep breath! "Good, I knew you would. Now, what I also need is for you and your band to be in costume. I was thinking of feathered masks, beads, and your attire. I need you to be in dramatic ball gowns, think Dangerous Liaisons, George and Martha Washington."

"That sounds like fun. I'm sure the band will enjoy being mysterious."

"That's the spirit."

I was just about to high-five her when the pain of holding a full bladder became too much to bear.
"Mrs. Mahoney, may I use your restroom?"

"Oh sure, go into the house and there is one off the main hall, next to the library."
"Thank you, I'll be right back."
I walked really fast and found the bathroom at last...

The white towels in the bathroom had a crest with the letter M embroidered on the front of them, just like a fancy hotel.
I whistled at the sight of marble that caved me in here, gold sinks and gold framed mirrors, classy, I could be comfortable in this.

I put on some lotion from the tray of complementary toiletries on the counter. A product from Europe written in French, and feeling like silk and scented with roses, wow!
I went out to the hallway that led to the library, which was enormous. Shelves were floor-to-ceiling with a movable ladder that was fastened to the bookshelf. The large fireplace with a mantel held a cigar box and an antique lighter.

Four wingback chairs in brown leather and a sofa furnished the room, and along the wall, a large oak bar with a brass rail on the bottom.

The large antique piece, probably from prohibition, I guessed, had racks for hanging glasses overhead. A copper blender sat behind it, waiting for someone to make a margarita or something fruity and yummy.

A shelf behind the bar held bottles of fine Tequila, Whiskey, Brandy, and Vodka. I felt like I was staring at the bar like a kid looking at a toy store.

"Would you like a drink?"

I turned around, startled, not realizing someone else was in the room with me.

Mr. Mahoney stood up from one of the wingback chairs that had been facing the other wall.

"Sure, thank you."

He walked over to the bar and grabbed a short glass.

"I'm sorry to barge in. I had to use the restroom, and I walked by the library. It caught my attention."

"Don't apologize, Ms. Rodriguez, it's quite all right," he smiled.

"So what'll it be, Scotch on the rocks, a Martini?"

"A Martini sounds great."

He opened a small fridge under the counter of the bar and took out a cold martini glass and some olives.

He busied himself with his task, which he seemed to enjoy.

"So you know who I am?"

"Of course, you're the gal that sings at Kendle's, your boyfriend is the fireman Lt. Stevens,"

he snapped his fingers, trying to recall Matt's name.

"Well, not anymore."

"Sorry to hear that," he said,

"Relationships are not my specialty." I said,

"I know how you feel. Here you are, this might make things better." he handed me the Martini.

"You look like a pro. Did you ever tend bar before?"

"As a matter of fact, I did. A job I had while I was at graduate school, it was a lot of fun, tending bar till 2 am, going to class at 10 am, and juggling sports, those were the days I was a broke college student living on Top Ramen and Oreos."

He laughed.

He seemed very content thinking of the simpler times in his life that brought him happiness.

"But you know what I think? It was the best time of my life," he said, looking back with happiness.

I could now see why Chanel had fallen hard for Mr. Mahoney; he was very charming, very easy to talk to, simple, laid back, almost like a free spirit.

He was pleasant and calm, the complete opposite of John Amos. Chanel felt safe with him; she felt comforted by his kindness.

"So, I guess congratulations are in order. I hear you're going to be running for Governor."

His face was somber, then he looked as though the good he would be able to do, and it seemed to make him feel better about his decision to run. "Maybe I can do some good for the entire state."

"Did you always want to be in politics?"

He took a drink of his Scotch.

"No, I wanted to be a writer, I love books as you can see."

He waved his arm around to show the vast collection on the shelves.
"I wanted to write novels about adventure, maybe in the mountains or
on the sea, like the classics, pirates, big ships, grizzly bears, 20,000
Leagues Under the Sea, or Hemingway, Treasure Island. Call of the
Wild, that sort."

"So what's stopping you now?" I asked.

He was silent for a moment, contemplating his answer or maybe
remembering something or someone else.

"I had a friend who thought just like you. Why wait. She said. Just do
it! Fulfill your dreams, I think it's your generation, Ms. Rodriguez. You

just do it, you don't sit around thinking about it or waiting for an

opportunity, you create one she would say." He finished his Scotch and
poured another.

I knew he was speaking of Chanel; the lost look in his eyes was sad and
longing.

"So go ahead, do it, enjoy your life, you deserve to be happy,"
I said.

He took another drink and poured another, his eyes glassy now, his
speech a little slurred, he started swaying a bit, the liquor taking effect,
no doubt.

"Mr. Mahoney, why don't you sit? You don't look so good."

"I'll be fine."

He walked around the bar, put his glass down, and headed for the door.

"Stay as long as you like. I think I'm going to hit the sack."

With that, he dropped to the floor.

I ran to help him up

"Mr. Mahoney, Mr. Mahoney, are you awake?"

His eyes opened a little; they were bloodshot, and he was disoriented. I helped him up and tried to get him to the couch.

With one arm over my shoulder, I walked him to the brown leather sofa and lay him out to rest.

I took off his shoes and put his legs on the sofa, and he snuggled up to his side.

"Thank you,"

He closed his eyes and mumbled a few things, and he was out like a light, snoring away the misery of his loss.

I felt so sorry for him; he seemed like a lost little boy running from his fears.

I left the library and closed the door behind me. I wanted to snoop around but thought better of it.

Outside, everyone was still rushing around making light of the demands coming from the Mrs.

I blended in with the crowd around the lawn and was not at all missed.

Everything and everyone was just as they were before I went searching for the lavatory.

I couldn't believe what I just heard from Mr. Mahoney. He was so distraught over Chanel.

Clearly, she had guided his choice for leaving politics, and his wife was the driving force to run; he wasn't really the one who wanted to be Governor.

Now with Chanel out of the way, wifey was pulling all of the strings, and she was moving as fast as a speeding train. I took my packet of info and decided to leave.

I had seen more than enough today.

Chapter 13

How About Lunch

On my way back from the Mayor's house, my phone rang; again, it said
PUBLIC. Not another crank call, I wondered. I picked up and prepared
for a heavy breather or a threat on my life. Instead, it was Detective
Anderson.

"Hi, I was wondering if you wanted to grab a late lunch."

It was 2 pm, and he was barely eating lunch; then again, I hadn't eaten
either.

"Okay, where do you want to go?"

A large Coke and two Baja tacos later, Detective Anderson and I were
on the subject of the mayor's birthday party.

The patio seating with tall red umbrellas provided shade to all the
outdoor diners, and the water misters cooled the skin in this 90-degree
sunshine.

"So you went to the mansion, huh?" Anderson asked,

"It was a hotel. Have you been there?"

"Yes, a few of the detectives went there last month for a mixer for the
Chamber of Commerce. Community relations it's part of the job."
He brushed it off like no big deal.

I wanted to talk about the murder, so I tried to slowly switch gears. "I had a great time last night."

"Me too, and thank you again for dinner last night."

"You're welcome." I blushed, recalling our time together. But then I came back to my senses.

"So are you guys finished with the "big" case? I asked using quotations to emphasize which case I was referring to.

"You mean Chanel O' Conner."

"Yes."

"The case is closed, we caught our guy, and now he's dead, the case is over." He seemed satisfied.

"Tell me something, let's say what if John Amos didn't do the crime, what if he was set up?"

"We had a confession. Why would he confess to something he didn't do?"

"Maybe he was put up to it."

"Who would do that?"

"I don't know, maybe there's more to this case than everyone thinks."

"Nikki, why are you so interested?" He was reading me now, his little psych degree going to work.

"I told you before, Chanel was a friend, and I just want to make sure you got the right person."

I pleaded with doe eyes, men can never resist them. Ha ha ha.

I thought about the journal and how I could tell him about the evidence in this case that he was missing.
"I can respect that, but honestly, all the evidence we have points to Amos."

"Okay, but what if you found more evidence that would give you a different lead? What would you do then?"
I couldn't tell if he was really buying it; he was hard to read, and it bugged the crap out of me.

"It depends on the evidence, whether or not it's sufficient to reopen the case. Look, I know you want to help Nikki, but I can do my job just fine. I wouldn't go to a party and try to tell you how to sing now, would I?"
I knew he had a point there, and now the defensiveness was showing through! He had *the* I'm not incompetent look.

But I had to admit I did find something that he didn't.
"Paul, I have to tell you something. Now you have to promise me that you won't." We were interrupted when his phone rang.

"It's the job, hold on. Anderson,"
He said, talking to the whip again.

"Okay, make sure you get a judge to sign it. I'm on my way."
He hung up the phone and got up from his seat.

"I'm sorry, I really have to go. We have this new lead on a 10-year-old case. How about dinner later tonight?"

"Okay, after practice, how about 7:30 pm?"

"Ok, see you." he kissed me and picked up his tray of food wrappers, tossed them in the trash, he got into his unmarked cruiser, and left.

CHAPTER 14

Guys, Guys, Please

It was 7 pm when the band left practice this evening. I gave them the lowdown on the party and the costumes we needed to wear.

Roxy asked if I had any plans for the evening. "Hey girl, what cha' doing tonight?"

"Dinner with a cop, how about you?"

"I'm going to see this new vampire movie; the guys in it are pretty sexy."

"I'm sure they are just your type, Roxy. Are you going alone?"

"No way, I got a new guy, he's not a Goth or a vamp, you wouldn't believe it."

"What happened to Vampire Man?"

"He went back to school, he left for Colorado last week, and anyway, we were just friends.

So this new guy, he's so hot, and his body is ripped, he's a personal trainer at LA Fitness."

Roxy and her hormones, geez, this girl!

"Hey, you never told me how your date went with Mr. Handcuffs."

"We had dinner at my place, we talked, and he's so easy to talk to. Roxy, I feel really good about him. We uh, you know, we spent the night together."

She smacked my arm.

"I knew it, ok details, is he hot?"

I just smiled and said, "We fell asleep on the patio, seriously, I'm taking it slow."

"Yeah, I get you. So does this mean you're over Fire Boy?"

I stared down at the ground, thinking.

"I think so. I mean, really, he's moved on, why can't I?"

I said, raising my head and feeling confident about my choice.

She looked at me in disbelief,

"I'd better head out, be good kay!" She tucked her box of drumsticks in her black bag and hugged me.

"Yeah, I'll see ya have fun at the movies."

"I'll tell you all about it tomorrow, so be up early for the details." She winked,

"Ok,"

"See ya,"

I closed the garage with the automatic garage door opener. Boy, was I hungry. I hope Paul doesn't cancel tonight. I really needed to tell him about the new info I had about the journal confirming Chanel and the Mayor's affair.

My phone chimed out a tune, and without thinking, I answered it.

"Hello,"

The voice on the other line was ruffled and distorted, and the moment it spoke, I felt rigid like a character in a Saw movie.

"I told you to stay away from Matt; he's mine, now you're going to pay."

The line went dead...

My eyes were as wide as can be, shocked, and I stood in fear. My low battery light was blinking wildly and ready to die any minute. I had to get back to my condo to call the police.

The summer sun was going down, and the evening blue skies were dimming to a dark raven.

I looked around for Roxy, but her car was gone already. My fear kicked in, and I ran from the garages and headed to the building of my condo, B-24. I passed the parking lot and carports that ran the length of the other buildings.

There weren't any cars coming or going as they usually are, but then again, it was dinner time, and people were either out for the night or home in front of their TVs.

I noticed not many windows were open as the night air had a slight chill coming from the east. For one thing, I also felt I wasn't alone. I looked behind me, but no one was there. Ok, Nikki, settle down, it's just your nerves.

I tried my calming yoga breathing to get me back to normal blood

pressure levels.

I came to the sidewalk, no one around, and quiet as a church, but just as I stepped up, headlights and a dark-colored car came from nowhere.

The bright headlights blazed towards me. I ran on the sidewalk, and the car followed me, now keeping pace with me along the road.

I had visions of a black-gloved hand coming from the driver's side window with a gun pointing in my direction. I shook it off in my mind and just kept going.

My heart was beating fast now, and I was using every athletic part of me to save myself from becoming a flat pancake on the floor.

I ran through a bunch of bushes and small trees. I could feel lashes and scrapes coming from the branches I tore past, fresh streaks of blood forming.

The car kept me from trying to get to the residential buildings by revving the engine and forcing me back to a corner. The only place to go was the clubhouse, which was to the right of me.

My best bet was to run in there and call the police; it had offices and a workout room, spa massage rooms, and a gourmet kitchen for the weekly cooking classes that were held there.

The pool was at the back of it, but after seven, the clubhouse was locked, and just my luck, no cooking class tonight.

I went around to the side entrance by the empty workout room and used my resident key to open the door. The car stopped, and a figure got out. I ran in and tried the second door from the weight room that led to the rest of the club.

The dark figure followed.

I ran to the front offices of the clubhouse, hoping just one door would be open. All the offices were locked for the day, no events in the dining room were held this evening, and the clubhouse was dark too.

I could hear footsteps closing in on me. I pulled out my cell phone and dialed 911.

"Please help me, I'm being chased by someone trying to kill me. I'm at

11267 Rancho Club View Dr. I'm in the clubhouse, hurry, call det.

Anderson tell him it's Nikki Rodriguez..." The cell went dead, no

battery! It was horrible. Oh, just my luck. Why didn't I charge it earlier

today? Damn!!

My breath was fast and coming in spurts, and my arms throbbed from

the bloody lashes given to me by the trees.

I ran around the club trying every door I could, but all were locked.

I ran to the massage room, my hands wet and shaking, gripped the door

handle, and finally an open door, I ran into the small room and closed

it. Thank God it had a lock on it.

The police would be here soon; they were coming. I'd be saved, oh,

hurry please, Paul, hurry.

I could hear someone running toward the room, they shook the door

handle, and not being able to open it, the dark figure stopped. I heard

the footsteps moving away fast!

Maybe they left, maybe the police are here. With relief flooding me, I

got up from my crouch on the floor and walked to the door, pressing

my ear against it to hear if the coast was clear.

Then a loud thud sent me falling back. Someone was hitting the door

with a hard object, and he or she was trying to get in.

I looked around the room searching for a weapon of any kind,

something, all I could find was a small bookshelf that had a few

candles and a lighter, some clean towels, and some robes.

Oh man, what do I do? The pounding was harder now; whoever was on

the other side wanted to hurt me badly.

I looked up at the ceiling, thinking of anything, then I thought of the lighter, the sprinkler. I grabbed the lighter from the small

wooden shelf, I held the lighter up to the sprinkler, and boom, they went off along with a loud alarm that all of Rancho Niguel could hear. I crouched behind the massage table, huddled in a corner of the room.

I said a few prayers begging for some help. I felt like Jamie Lee Curtis in Halloween when Mike Myers was hacking away at the closet she was hiding in.

The wood splintered on the door. I could see a partial view of the dark figure, holding an ax, all dressed in black. The lock on the door jammed, but my attacker gave it another hit, and with another thunk. I

screamed! A loud, blood-curdling sound, but then the dark figure froze. The sirens were wailing now and very close; help was on the way. My attacker gave me one final look and ran off!
I got up from the floor, my legs shaking like Jell-O, as I tried to pry the door open. I heard footsteps, several of them getting closer. The door was stuck, so I kicked it twice, and it fell open.

The Cavalry was here: police, fire, and rescue. I dropped to the floor, in pain.
Detective Anderson was the first one in, with Matt and his team right behind him.

They ran to me at the same time,
"Are you okay?" they said in unison.
The alarm had stopped ringing, but my head didn't.
I was out of breath.

153

"I'm not hurt, but someone tried to kill me; they ran out through the weight room door."

"I'm going to check the perimeter, go with Lt. Stevens."

Anderson had his gun out, and he went to catch the perp who tried to kill me.

"Can you walk?"

"Yeah." I was wet from head to toe and was now starting to shake.

Matt picked me up and carried me out of the building to an ambulance waiting outside.

I sat on a gurney with a blanket over my shoulders while the medics cleaned my bare arms from the bloody scratches.

Matt took off his hat and coat and sat next to me.

"How are you feeling?"

"Better."

"You're never a dull moment, Nikki!"

"Thanks."

"I guess this is twice I've had to come to your place for an emergency call."

"Hey, I didn't plan either one."

"I'm just glad you're okay," he said seriously.

"Matt, I got one of those weird phone calls just before I was attacked."

"What calls?"

Paul made his appearance.

"Are you all right? When I got the call, I was already on my way here. What happened?"

Matt and Paul were quiet while I spilled out my entire story about the strange calls I'd been getting and the one I got right before the attack. Paul jotted down all the info in his little black standard-issue notebook. Matt looked distressed.

Anderson spoke first, "So Summer Simons received threatening calls, and she thought you made them, but you received the calls thinking she made them."

"Yes, and the location on the phone said PUBLIC. Do you think you can get the phone records and trace the call?"

"That shouldn't be a problem, but if they are coming from a public line, we might not know who made them; we'll just have a location on it."

"Well, it's a start."

"I'll need to have a word with Ms. Simons and get her records as well."

"Summer wouldn't do this, she's not that kind of person," Matt said, sticking up for her.

"You were okay with blaming me for it in the grocery store." I spat back.

"No, Nikki, I never thought..."

"Sure you did!" I interrupted.

"No, what I thought was that you were...

"Don't say anything, Matt."

I threw off the blanket and jumped off the gurney, and walked over to Paul

"Weren't we supposed to have dinner and drinks tonight?" I asked him

"If you're feeling up to it, I still have more questions for you,"

"She needs to rest, she's been through a lot, and someone tried to kill her tonight." Matt said

"With me, she'll have police protection," Paul said,

"She was given a sedative no drinks, besides I think she needs to go home and get some rest." Matt said standing tall.

"Well she hasn't had dinner yet and I think she needs something in her stomach," Paul responded.

"I'm off in an hour I'll cook her dinner." Matt said which

surprised me, didn't he have to go to see miss pretty princess?

I stood between Mr. Anderson and Mr. Stevens's pissing contest here, it was like one each held an arm of mine and started pulling, I had to end this!

"All right that's enough, Matt I'm going home, Detective I'll call in some dinner from Magiano's, they deliver, and you can ask me all the questions you need too, all right."

They both pulled themselves together,

"That's fine with me." Paul said

He took his sports jacket off and placed it on my shoulders
Matt walked over to me,

"Honey I'll come by first thing in the morning and check on you."

He kissed me on the cheek and went back to his fire truck.

The audience of Fire and Rescue and the Police Department parted and turned as if they were minding their own business the whole time and didn't just witness an episode of The Young and the Restless!

They all packed it up and drove off.

Paul and I walked to my condo

"I thought he wasn't your boyfriend?"

"He's not. We broke up."

"Think again, darling, looks like I have competition."

CHAPTER 15

Dear Diary

I woke up to the smell of maple bacon cooking. I opened my eyes and tried to focus on the numbers on my clock. 8:30 am
I yawned, got up and went to the shower. I let the hot water run all over, boy did it feel good on my aching body.

My arms were sore from the scratches and bruises that I got from running for my life.
I had tossed and turned last night over the thought of why someone would want to kill me. Was it the diary? No one knew I had it except Roxy, Martin, and Oliver.
The dark car could have been the same one following Chanel, it could also be the same person who was in the condo that night I found the diary. Maybe someone did see me coming out, but then why not attack me there and then?
I got dressed, put on my makeup, and went to the kitchen.
Matt was cooking up a feast, bacon, scrambled eggs, and pancakes with chocolate chips. The man could cook I'd give him that.
"Good morning Sunshine." he said handing me a cup of coffee
"Good morning, how did you get in here?" I asked him
"I still have my key, do you want it back?"
he asked dangling the brass in front of me.

"No, for safety reasons I mean it's good for someone I trust to have it."

I said taking a sip of Beach Break roast coffee

"So what did Detective Anderson ask you about last night?"

Wow so much interest all of a sudden what was Matt's game here

Was he jealous of seeing Paul take me home and having an evening alone with me?

"The usual, do I have any enemies, or have I made anyone angry with me lately, I told him in detail about the calls and what the caller sounded like."

"Do you think it's Summer doing this to you?" He handed me a plate of heavenly-smelling food.

He was very cautious with his tone of voice not sounding too accusatory or negative.

"I don't know Matt," I said taking the plate and sitting down at the table.

He served himself a cup of coffee and came to the table, set down his cup, and said

"She's not that type."

I took a bite of my delicious chocolate chip pancakes, dripping with butter and syrup.

"Matt, all I know is that someone came after me."

"Do you have an enemy out there?"

I thought about telling Matt about the journal and my suspicion that someone was on my tail to get the information in it.

"Enemies no nothing comes to mind." I lied

"I just want to say I'm sorry I accused you of making those phone calls to Summer. Obviously, I wasn't thinking."

"I forgive you. Is that why you're here out of guilt?" I asked stuffing more pancakes into my mouth.

"No, I'm here because I'm your friend." He smiled.

The doorbell rang, and at this hour, I had no idea who it could be.

"Are you expecting anyone?"

"No," I said, surprised.

Matt got up and went to the door to answer it.

"Detective Anderson, what brings you here?" The two men looked at each other with annoying glances.

"Morning everyone," he said passing Matt and coming to the table to have a seat.

"I've got some news on your stalker."

"What did you find out?" I asked,

"Well, we traced the calls from your cell phone and from Ms. Simmons's cell phone, and the public number came from City Hall.

"City Hall!"

I blurted out.

Paul shook his head to confirm,

"To my understanding, Ms. Simmons works for the city in the

Purchasing department at City Hall, correct?" He asked, turning to Matt for a response. "Yes, that's the department she works for."

Matt said, confirming,

"Okay, now in the City Hall building, there are at least a dozen phones in each department and a set of four public phones in the lobby.

The calls came from a pay phone in the lobby, a phone in Parks and Recreation, and two calls from the Human Resources department. Now, Matt, I hate to be the bearer of bad news, but your girlfriend works there, and she has opportunity and motive."

"How can you say that?" Matt asked,
"I spoke with Kiana Zane, she is a co-worker with Ms. Simmons, she also lives here at the condo complex, and she's a friend of yours, Nikki."

"Yes, I went to high school with her husband, Craig, you know, Craig, he's a cop, here in Rancho Niguel."

"Yes, I know Craig and Kiana. Anyway, she told me that she spoke to Ms. Simmons at her candle party a few days ago, and Ms. Simmons was very upset with Nikki. She mentioned to Kiana that Nikki's presence has caused quite a rift in her relationship with Matt."
Matt didn't seem surprised, but I was.
"What else did Kiana say?" I asked,
"She mentioned the phone calls, she said Ms. Simmons was very upset by them, and she was a little freaked out, and she asked Matt to tell you to leave her alone ."

"The thing is, I didn't make any of those calls to her."

"I know you didn't, that's why we're going to bring Ms. Simmons in for questioning."

"She didn't do any of this; someone's setting her up."
Matt said,
"Maybe Matt, but who would do that?" Anderson replied.

This was a good time as any I had to give the journal to Paul
I got up from the table and went to my room to retrieve it.

While the two men defended their views on the subject.
I lifted my mattress and fished out the journal. I walked back to the
living room and handed off the evidence.

"Here, this is why someone was trying to hurt me last night, and I don't
know if it has anything to do with the calls."
I handed Paul the journal.

"What's this?"

"It's Chanel O' Conner's journal"

He flipped through the journal, skimming the words on the pages and
looking like a kid on Christmas.
"Where did you get this?"
I thought fast,

"That's classified, I can't tell you that."

"How long have you had it?" Matt asked

"I can't tell you that."

"What's with all the secrets, Nikki?" Matt asked a little annoyed
I ignored his question

"Paul do you think that you can re-open the case?"

"Absolutely."

He was still reading some of the pages of new information I had given
him.
"This is beautiful Nikki but I need to know how did you get this and
who else knows about it?"

"I came upon it."

"Where Nikki?" Matt demanded

They were both looking at me with stern faces demanding an answer. All of a sudden they were tag teaming me like a WWF wrestler wanting to know how and when, where, and why I had found this piece of evidence

"I ... I found it."

"Nikki if someone knows you have this book chances are they will try to kill you to get it," Paul said

I was caving and I couldn't keep up the charade any longer.

"I ... okay I went into Chanel's Condo a week ago and I found it under a floorboard and then someone else came into the condo while I was there and I hid in the shower, whomever it was came looking for the journal. When they left I got out of there and came home, that's the truth."

Paul ran his hand over his mouth in disbelief, and Matt just stood with his jaw open in awe.

They were quiet for what seemed like forever but in reality only two seconds.

"You went into a crime scene, and searched for clues with a killer on your ass?" Paul barked out

"I was just trying to help."

"Nikki do you think I don't know how to do my job." he was angry now.

"No, Paul, I just thought maybe there was something you missed."

"I could arrest you right now for tampering with evidence and keeping it from me. And let's see breaking and entering and a hoard of other things you've done."

"I didn't break in I found a key under the big plant by the door."

"Oh, my God." Paul said pacing the room

Matt had made a few chuckles

"I think you should haul her ass in." Matt said,

"I think I'll take your advice." Paul said,

"I may be guilty of snooping around and all that other stuff you said but I just gave you the biggest lead in your case."

 I said,

"You're going to get yourself killed." Matt said,

"I'm putting you under protective custody, someone knows you have this and I can guarantee you they will be back."

Paul took out his cell phone

"This is Detective Anderson, I need to have a 24-hour watch on Ms. Nikki Rodriguez, follow her everywhere she goes, don't let her out of your sight, and protect her at all costs."

He hung up his phone and headed for the front door.

"Whatever you do today keep an eye out for anyone suspicious and call me if anything new surfaces."

After he left I picked up the dishes and started packing the dishwasher. Matt started cleaning the counters for me

He was pretty quiet I guess he was just taking in everything that was going on.

"I have a lot to do today, thank you for breakfast and for coming by to check on me I appreciate it."

"I don't understand why you couldn't come to me with any of this."

"Matt you're not available to me like that anymore."

"Nikki..."

His phone rang again

He answered it and spoke

"Hello Summer"

I walked back to my room to get my shoes and my purse, and when I came back into the living room, Matt was off the phone.

"That was Summer she really needs me right now, and Anderson has to question her"

"Go ahead Matt you don't have any obligation to me, it's not like I'm asking you to stay."

"Why do you act like this?"

"I don't know what you're talking about," I said searching for my keys.

"You act like you don't give a damn about me, you're the one that didn't want the obligation to me."

"You're right Matt I didn't want to be obligated by someone that every girl in Rancho Niguel was after, how could I trust you!"

"I told you I never cheated on you, I never looked at another girl when we were together, for God's sake I asked you to move in with me, does that sound like someone who's going to cheat on you?

Just admit it you're afraid of commitment, it's not me it's you, no strings attached, isn't that what you said when we first went out."

"Why are you so upset you're free to do what you want, I didn't trap you."

"I never thought of you trying to trap me, I want to be with you, plain and simple."

He took his car keys from the coffee table and left.

CHAPTER 16

Hello Det. Diaz

My first stop was the costume shop on Sunflower Way,
The girls of Little Black Dress filled the small dressing rooms, with
dresses of every color of the rainbow. Flouncing around in yards of
fabric; lace, satin, sparkle, and lots of petticoats. We settled on
One Orange, one hot pink, an emerald green, a rich red, and a royal
purple. Along with matching garters and long-sleeved gloves, we
looked like we were ready for Mardi Gras. The security people came by
the condo just before I left to collect the IDs and said I would be able to
have them by 4:30 pm.

I set up an extra practice for this evening to go over the songs for Mr.

Mahoney's party and to give the girls their passes.

After lunch, Roxy and I went to the mall to buy some red shoes to
match my red ball gown.

"They have to be flashy, we're talking Mardi Gras here," Roxy said as
we looked over all the high heels in Macy's.

"Of course, I wouldn't want anything different,"

I told her trying on a pair of glittered black strappy stilettos. "So tell me
what happened last night, you started your story, and then bam you

167

froze up. What gives?"

"Oh, Roxy you wouldn't believe what happened."

I told her about the attack on me and the big pissing contest between my former boyfriend and my latest one, yada yada, and twenty minutes later, I wrapped up my story.
"Your life is just too much fun." she laughed

"Yeah and dangerous." I said,

"I think it's erotic, two guys fighting over you, a murderer out for your head, and a case you're trying to solve, and it's exciting."
"Oh yeah with Matt talking about my commitment issues and why we broke up or should I say why I broke us up exciting."
"Come on you know what I mean."

"Yeah, but he's right it was my fault, I do have a problem when it comes to the whole living together or God the big word I can't even say it the M word."
"Not all Marriages end in bitter divorce like your parents."
"Roxy my parents were married for 25 years, loved each other, and then my dad cheated, lied, broke my mom's heart, and then was killed tragically. It's like one of those sad movies that ends without a happy ending! I just feel like I'm doomed for failure already."
"I'm sorry Nikki I know you had a crap shoot but you can be happy too! Everyone is responsible for their own happiness."

"I'm not ready to face that yet, I need more time. I'm more focused on my future career. Besides I'm too busy right now and did I mention that I have my own security, around me like a celebrity." Changing the mood from somber to silly I discreetly pointed to a guy in a suit standing off to the side of the shoe department.

"No way, you're under police protection now, it's cool, he's cute." She said sizing him up.

"Oh, what do you think of these," I said holding up a pair of cute Carlos Santana heels in shiny red glitter.

"Sexy, take them!"

They were perfect and they would go with several things in my closet as well.

"So tell me girly which one are you going to choose?"

"The red heels."

She tsk'd with annoyance

"No, that's not what I mean?"

"I choose my career."

Roxy laughed and held up a pair of black heels with a glittery spider web design.

"I'm so getting these," she said blowing them a fake kiss with her big red lips.

"They are definitely you."

After Macy's, Roxy and I had a coffee at Starbucks or (Buckie's) as she usually calls them, then she went off to see her latest love and I was on my way home.

Along the way I passed Kendle's, the place was simmering down from the lunch crowd; some of the bus boys were hanging outside In the back taking cigarette breaks and throwing quarters at the wall. The one busboy with the tattoo on his hand was talking to Kaid, it looked like they were arguing, then Kaid walked off. The busboy walked to the parking lot and got into an old 1960s Impala and drove off.

I ran over to the restaurant to look for Kaid, I searched the Lobby, then I asked the usual hostess/Manager Donna, where he was. "He's up in his office Nikki go right up," she said. My police detail following a few paces beside me came in with me but waited in the kitchen.

I went up the spiral stairs to Kaid's office, his receptionist was gone and he was alone.

Kaid was sitting at his desk filing some papers when I walked in. "Kaid I'm sorry to bother you but I was across the street and I couldn't help but notice that you seemed so upset, are you okay."

"Nikki, don't worry it was nothing, hey are you ready for the Mayor's birthday bash this weekend?" he went back to filing.

"Yes, from what I saw it looks to be the best party I've seen around here."

"I think so too."

I didn't know if I should pry but I needed more to go on, for Paul to have a solid case. So I pushed a little harder.

"Kaid are you in some kind of trouble?" I asked innocently

He looked up from his work, a worried expression on his face.

"What are you talking about Nikki?"

"Kaid does it have anything to do with Chanel O' Conner?"

He stood up and walked around from the desk his expression from
worry went to anger. Yikes, I hit a nerve!

"All right who are you working for?" he asked grabbing my arm, his
laid-back surfer attitude gone, now replaced with a paranoid
and scared-looking stranger.

"I'm not working for anybody Kaid honest." he was hurting me now
gripping my arm tighter.

"Then how do you know about my problem with Chanel?"

"I know that she was blackmailing you." he let go of me, and I wanted
to bolt but my curiosity got the best of me.

He sat on the corner of his desk, searching for an answer

"Yes she was blackmailing me, but I swear I didn't kill her."

"Did you kill John Amos?"

"No I didn't Nikki." he was looking me straight in the eyes and I knew
he was telling me the truth.

"I'm sorry I didn't mean to scare you by grabbing your arm."

He said apologizing.

Then I pushed a little harder

"I know about the R.I. Pioneers, were you a drug lord or a dealer?"

He gave an I don't know what you're talking about look

But I beat him to the point

"Don't say you have no idea what I'm talking about!"

171

He shrugged his shoulders and gave in. The laid-back surfer Dude was back.

"I was a dealer for the Rhode Island Pioneers, a group of five guys that took over the drugs on the east coast, I was their head dealer, I hated what I did I wanted to get out, but I didn't know how. Then one night I went out to make a buy, at a warehouse I had four other guys with me and 10 million dollars in two briefcases, the deal went south, everyone brought out guns, and bullets started flying everywhere, so I grabbed the money and ran." He stared off to the right, giving up his story like a criminal that has been caught. He focused on the window panes of his office, pushing himself to let out this secret he had been caring with him for so long.

He waved his hands in the air mimicking explosions going off.
"It was a war zone, a grenade went off, and the whole place went up in smoke, I was able to get away, I jacked a car and drove the whole night. I got as far away as I could, it was my chance out. When I read the morning papers it said that everyone had died in the fire, they all thought I died and that the money went up in smoke." His eyes were watery begging for my understanding and my help in keeping his secret.
"I changed my name, dyed my hair blond, bought some green contact lenses, and came out here to Southern California to make a new start. Everything was going well, I had my life back." He smiled as if he had been redeemed.
"Then that bastard John Amos, he was a junkie slash dealer from back east, he saw me one night and I don't know how but he knew who I was.

He said he wanted money or else he would rat me out to the R.I. Pioneers. They would have killed me! So I decided I was going to pay him off, but then he got arrested.

I thought my troubles were over then Chanel came to me and did the same thing. She seemed desperate and cold like she needed this as a way out. I guess I could have gone to the police or the FBI, but I just wanted to be done with all of this so I just gave her the money and told her to keep her mouth shut.

She agreed, she said she was leaving town anyway, and I'd never have to worry about her again.

The next thing I know she ends up dead and then a few weeks later Amos is dead. Here I'm thinking I get my life back!

Then you come around asking questions." he folded his arms over his chest.

"So what do you want Nikki, how much to keep you quiet."

"I don't want your money Kaid, I just want to know who killed Chanel

and why is someone trying to kill me now."

"Someone's trying to kill you, who and why?" he looked puzzled

"That's what I want to know," I said crossing my arms over my chest.

"Sorry Nikki I can't stay and help you, I can't take a chance that John and Chanel didn't rat me out, so I'm leaving." he went behind the desk and picked up a very expensive piece of luggage.

"Don't worry the restaurants will stay open, I just won't be here."

"Wait Kaid what if you go to the police or the FBI they can help you in exchange for putting these drug kings away and you'll never have to run again."

"Are you crazy I would get killed as it is I'll be looking over my shoulder the rest of my life?"

"How long are you going to keep running Jack Mendel?"

He looked at me in disbelief

"Darling I'm not even going to ask you how you found that out, are you sure you're not a cop or the FBI."

"She isn't but I am."

We both turned around, the bus boy with the tattoo, two suits, and Detective Anderson stood behind Us.

"Agent Dominguez FBI," the tattoo man held up his badge

"What the hell is this, how did you find me?"

"Kaid or should I say, Donnie Ferrelli, we've been tailing you for a year now, Agent Dominguez kept watch on the inside and when Detective Anderson brought us the information from Chanel O' Conner's diary, we moved in." one of the suits said.

"Hey I didn't kill anybody, I'm not into dealing anymore, and I run a clean place."

"We know that we want you to testify against the R.I pioneers, you'll have federal protection, and you won't do any jail time as long as you cooperate."

Kaid (Donnie or Jack), whoever he was today, sat down at his desk to think of the deal the feds were offering him.

"They'll kill me and if they don't I'll be looking over my shoulder the rest of my life just what I told Nikki here." he said,

"Not if you're in the witness protection program they won't even know you're testifying we can protect your identity, we will have to relocate you, it's not safe here anymore."

Kaid thought about it for a minute, contemplating all the possibilities of what he was going to give up and change in his life for helping the feds lock up these felons that were poisoning our country. He shook his head back and forth, maybe yes, maybe no, then he put his arms up in defeat. "I don't have a choice, do I? Just one thing, don't send me anywhere with ice and snow."

He agreed to it, Kaid cleaned out his desk and made arrangements for his businesses to be sold, and all the other technicalities were to be discussed in private.

"So long, Kaid, good luck."

"Take care, butterfly," he waved.

The feds took him out the back door of the kitchen and that was the last time I ever saw Kaid Kendle.

Anderson and I were the last ones in the office
"So are you still mad at me?" I asked him
"I'm not mad at you, but how the hell do you keep popping up everywhere."

"This is my town," I said, flirting.

CHAPTER 17

New Evidence

Detective Anderson put his black shades on the clean white countertop where we sat drinking milkshakes at Johnny Rockets.

The place was empty, the jukebox was playing a nice tune by The Platters, "Smoke Gets In Your Eyes."

Okay, I admit I love oldies, I grew up listening to them and I sing them, you have to love what you do.

"So did you find out anything new on the case?" I asked,

"You know I can't tell you anything."

"Ok but tell me, is the journal helping?"

"It's bringing up a lot of questions."

He took a drink of his milkshake.

"Do you think Mrs. Mahoney is a suspect?"

"It's hard to say we have no evidence that she was at the condo that day,

the only prints in the condo were Chanel's."

"What about Mr. Mahoney, he had an affair with her, where was he the afternoon she was killed?"

He looked tired but counted off his reasons one by one, his bright

watercolor blue/green eyes vivid with life even though he was winding down.

"First he denied the affair, he said nothing like that ever happened. Next, he said he was out of the office, at the mall purchasing a gift for his wife."

"Does he have any witnesses to verify that?"

"Not yet."

"How can he deny what's in the journal, does he think that she just made everything up? "

"He denied the affair we didn't give him the details of the journal." "He was in the area he had access and motive, from what Chanel wrote in the journal he could've backed out of their plans, and then she could've threatened him by telling his wife or going to the press, she could have ruined him politically right."

"It adds up to a lot of maybes and pure speculation my dear." He took a long drink of his shake, inhaling the rush of sugar.

I thought of what Marge had told me at Kiana's candle party, the part about Chanel going off with an older man and moving away from a bad marriage. I thought about telling Paul to go off and question Marge, but then I figured I better not. Instead, I asked him a question.

"So he doesn't know about the journal?"

"No, As soon as we mentioned the affair, he threatened to call his lawyer and sue us. We did find the safe deposit box with a ring and the money that she took from Kaid, it will be placed in evidence."

"So then there is truth to the journal, isn't that enough proof."

"She could have been in love with the mayor, yes, but maybe in her mind they had something and that's what a lawyer would argue, there is no proof we have nothing."

"What about the ring?"

"It could have been from someone else unless we have a receipt with the mayor's name on it or his credit card number, then it would lead us in that direction, otherwise, nothing."

I played all the evidence in my mind trying to find a way to connect Mahoney to Chanel and the affair.

"Try looking into the conferences he attended with her,"

I told Paul looking hopeful.

"I'll see what I can do."

"Ok," I said with some hope then I asked him "She was sexually assaulted who did that?"

"Well the lab report on that came back and she was with John Amos, prior to her death, not to mention his confession, his suicide, case closed."

"But in the journal, Chanel mentioned that Mrs. Mahoney threatened her."

"It's here say, she could have made that up or misunderstood it, there's no proof sunshine."

"So the Mayor and his wife walk and that's it."

"Look I'm going to find something, trust me ok."

"Ok"

"Well what about my case, did you find out if Summer is behind the phone calls and the attack?"

"I interviewed her, with Matt right next to her.

She doesn't know any more than you do, and she has an alibi for last night, and there are no dents or scrapes on her white Honda Civic.

My opinion is, I think both of you are being stalked by someone that's

head over heels on Mr. Calendar boy, so you're still on police protection."

"You mean someone wants Summer and me out of the picture?"

"You got it."

"A crazy fan?"

He shook his head

"I don't know, but I'm going to find out."

CHAPTER 18

Surfs Up

Saturday was finally here, the weather today would be sunny, with a high of 85 for mid-July, cool in the evening, and a low would be a balmy 65.

Yesterday Paul and I went to the beach. I didn't have my police detail today because I had Paul as my personal bodyguard. He said he had a surprise for me and that I had to wear a bathing suit.
Hmm, do I detect surfing?

We ended up in Huntington Beach; Paul parked his truck on PCH along with all of the other surfers. It wasn't too crowded yet, which was a relief for me.
"This is for you. " Paul handed me a box.

"What's this?" I asked,

"Open it."

"Oh my gosh, it's a wet suit."

"I believe it's your size."

It was wow, "this is great thank you." It was black and grey with

O'Neill written in baby blue on the front of it. Short-sleeved and covered to the knees it had a long zipper down the back.

He carried our boards to the sand and we camped and dropped our blanket and towels.

I opted for a black tankini and a ponytail today and lots of sunblock. I suited up in my new wet suit, I felt official now just like a real surfer girl. He gave me a crash course in land surfing (meaning you learn how to balance on the board before you have to stand to ride the wave. He showed me how to position my feet and what to do when I start to ride the wave. We headed for the ocean, caring my board I felt scared and excited at the same time.

"Are you ready?"

"Hmmm." My stomach did flip flops but I pushed it aside and smiled brightly.

"Let's do it!"

"Come on, you'll be fine."

We rode our boards on our bellies in the shallow water and started to paddle out.

"This is already amazing, Paul."

Gliding through the salty blue water, I felt all of my fear subsiding. The cool, refreshing ocean was calm at this point, but I could see several waves moving in the ocean, building up to a large wave.

"This is nothing, the best is yet to come, okay, now turn around the way I showed you."

"Ok, I got it." I listened to Paul's voice and kept balance with my body.

"All right, now when the wave comes, don't forget to paddle towards the beach when the wave starts to come."

The salty air was thick, spraying in my face a cool mist. The breeze off the ocean sent a slight chill down my back. I was glad to have the wet suit to keep me warm.
"Here we go."

I felt the water come under the board, pushing me forward like a rolling pin kneading bread. Here it was the wave, now I would have to try to stand just the way Paul taught me.
"Okay now balance yourself and ride the wave."

"Oh my gosh."

"You can do it just keep your balance."
I stood up and balanced perfectly, and then I rode the small wave...
We did this a few more times, Paul was experienced and he surfed just like a pro.
We were shooting the curl (surfer talk) I wiped out a few times but I got back on my board and went out again. After quite a few times I was beginning to get familiar with the water and what to do. I had never felt so amazing and so scared in one moment, it was the most exhilarating experience I have ever had.
Finally exhausted and worn down we ran back onto the sand and dropped our boards. My wet feet collected all the sand between my toes as we sloshed back to dry off and take a breath from what felt like running a marathon for hours.
"Oh my God, it was the most unbelievable moment in my life, So this is what I've been missing."

"I knew you could nail this, you're a natural."

"Yeah, but I wiped out a few times."

"You did well."

He spun me around in his arms, thrilled with my accomplishment.
It was such a rush, I felt like Sandra Dee in Gidget when she shouted
out "It positively surpasses every living emotion I've ever had." It was
the closest thing to flying, like a bird but in the ocean, ok maybe more
like a gliding dolphin, what can I say I felt like I was on top of the
world.
We went for a walk on the beach and talked about surfing the big waves
of Hawaii, he's been to Oahu and Maui but he said we had to get to
Australia one of these days.

Surfing music blared out from a small taco hut that we passed, there
were girls in black bikinis passing out flyers for a local competition
next week. Paul grabbed a flyer
"If I enter this contest will you come out here to cheer me on?"

"Yes I will, I'll come in my bikini."

"Sounds like a plan." He smiled.

We walked on and found seashells and sea glass in the sand. Skipped a
few rocks on the ocean and took in the late sun. A little bit of seaweed
and some sand had just washed up to our ankles.
I picked up the few light green pieces of sea glass lying among the

debris of rocks and broken seashells in the sand.
"I just love this stuff, it's so pretty."

"It is cool, so this is what happens when glass is washed in the ocean?"
Paul asked,

"Oh yeah, people make jewelry from this stuff; they use gold and silver, and sometimes diamonds, and it sells for a lot of money."
I stuffed them in the pocket of my shorts. For dinner, we were both craving burgers, so we hopped in the truck and went to my favorite burger joint. Now, even if you're not a Californian, you can appreciate this place.

We ordered cheeseburgers of course from In N' Out (a California landmark for making the best burgers and fries fresh not frozen and oh yeah did I mention the shakes, the burgers are filled with fresh 100% beef, real cheese, lettuce, fresh tomato, and secret sauce and fresh onion, or you can have it animal style which means a cheeseburger with grilled onions. There is this whole-off menu, menu that only Californians or die-hard fans know about. They have a double-double, two beef patties or a 4x4, meaning four beef patties, a little too much protein for me, but who am I to deny any other carnivore for what they want to consume? My fav is the double-double protein, in So Cal, that means a cheeseburger with double meat, tomato, and special sauce with lettuce wrapped around it, no bun. So, since the late 1940s, from a small burger stand in Baldwin Park, California, the In-N-Out Burger was born.)

We sat outside patio dining, each of us eating our burgers and savoring every bite.

"We should plan a trip to Hawaii one of these days since you haven't been there, then we could go to some of the most famous beaches for surfers Hanalei Bay Kauai, Jaws Maui, Laniakea Oahu, there are so many great spots."

"Oh and we have to go to a luau, I want to see those dancers that twirl the fire."
I had told him.
"Ok."

He said sitting close to me
The smell of his aftershave and his In N' out burger with no onions was driving me crazy.
I put a little distance between us and said
"When are we going to Hawaii?"

"Whenever you want." He said and smiled.

We went back to the beach for a bonfire, a small one, and roasted a few marsh mellows for s'mores, then took a midnight stroll that ended in a long kiss to the sound of crashing waves...

I was brought back to the present by the ring of my cell phone.
I ran to the kitchen where I had left my purse on the breakfast bar. I rummaged through my clutch handbag and retrieved my cell just in

time before it went to voice mail.
"Hello"

"Hi Nikki it's Oliver, do you have time for breakfast this morning."
I looked at the clock on the microwave, 8 am it read in green numbers.
"I have time, where do you want to meet?"

"Pastries of Paris in the courtyard across from the gallery."

Of course, for the best crepes in this town, many people went to Pastries of Paris.

Matt and I would spend lazy Sunday mornings having breakfast. Saturday nights when he was available we would go to the beach in San Diego and get dinner at Felipe's, the best pizza this side of the Mississippi, Matt and I would always say that we would try to make it off to Italy someday.

We are both food people, it's a good thing we both exercise insistently otherwise well let's just say it wouldn't be good. Matt and I had made a lot of travel plans that now have flown away in the wind.
I dismissed my daydream and answered Oliver's invitation.

"Ok, I'll be there in half an hour."
I put on a pair of jeans and a strapless yellow terry cloth top, my sunglasses, and my clutch purse, and I was running out the door. My police escort got out of his car and headed my way.
"I'm Officer Diaz. I'm sorry I didn't introduce myself sooner."

"Hi"

"I'll be with you every day until we find the perp that's stalking you."
He was a young officer about my age young 30s, with dark hair, dimples, and a nice smile, cool black sunglasses very Mario Lopez."

"Okay well, I'm going to the mall to meet some friends for breakfast."

"Just go about your business, as usual, Ms. Rodriguez, and it's nice to finally meet you."

"Oh thank you likewise." So I headed out me and my shadow.

"Hi, Nikki, hey Diaz," Craig said, walking to the pool with his sunblock and beach towel.
Mario Lopez just waved,
"Hi Craig, working on your tan in this heat?" I asked.

"No, I do 10 laps in the pool every day, it keeps me in shape."
He said patting his stomach wall.
"Have a good swim," I said trying to make a fast getaway. Although he wasn't going to let me go yet.

"Hey, so I hear you and Anderson are an item?"

"Where did you hear that?" I stopped dead in my tracks

"Nikki good news travels fast in this town, right Diaz." he said chuckling
Officer Diaz just nodded
"I hate to disappoint you but we're not an item, we're just friends." He gave me a sly look, eyebrow arched high as though he was guessing my game.
"Why? Are you still hung up on Matt?"

"Why would you say that?"

"He was at your apartment yesterday, right?"

"That's none of your business!" I said annoyed at his comment now.

"C'mon Nikki I just want to know which one you're going to pick, me and the guys at the station have a pool going."

"What!" I said in complete horror.

"Yeah, it's up to six hundred bucks, so tell me which one because I have two more days until I can change my answer."

"Oh, my God."

I walked away in disbelief leaving Craig to shrug his shoulders saying "Okay well maybe later."

I walked to the mall to go and stomach my crepes...

Martin and Oliver were in their usual slacks and silk shirts, already sipping espressos when I arrived.

"Hey, how's the world of art?" I asked taking a seat and setting my purse down on the table.

Officer Diaz stood to the side of the patio, guarding, and no words.

"Hi Nikki, it's busy you know there are so many new businesses in town and they all need art for their lobbies," Oliver said between sips of his espresso.

"Not to mention we donated a piece for the pancake breakfast auction."

Martin said,

"Oh yeah, I'm going to the breakfast. Which painting did you two

donate?"

"Killer Cool Jazz." Martin smiled.

"You mean I actually have a chance to bid on it?"

"Yes, we're starting the bidding at $500," Oliver said

"It will bring in a lot more than that. " I commented
I ordered a petite strawberry crepe and a vanilla café latte, with a side of fruit.
The 17-year-old waitress in her black Capri's and black and white stripe shirt took my order, her black beret slipped from her head.
"You dropped your hat."

"That darn thing has been bugging me all day," she said
She put her hat back in her pocket and went off.
"So tell me what's up?" Martin said nodding to Officer Diaz
"Officer Diaz is my bodyguard."

Martin and Oliver seized up Officer Diaz, a smile on Oliver's face saying he approved of my new shadow.

I filled them in on the brush with danger from the previous days, the close call by the clubhouse, and the chilling phone call that made my skin crawl every time I spoke to someone about it. I told them about the rivalry between Matt and Paul, the day at the beach, and the case of Kaid and the FBI. By the end of the conversation and the end of my crepes, their mouths had dropped to the floor.
"You're so like Charlie's Angels, Nikki, how do you get into these things?" Oliver asked

"I think it's the men you hang out with," Martin said, pulling out his Italian leather wallet and putting down the platinum Amex.

"Oh yeah, and did I tell you it's official I have a stalker?"

"Play Misty For Me?" Oliver asked.

"No, the stalker is after Summer too!"

After breakfast, we walked back to the art gallery

"Ok so I was going to ask you what our next move was for questioning Mahoney but it looks like you've got your hands full Nikki." Oliver said holding the door open for me as we walked into the gallery.

"No I have my police guard to watch me and don't worry as of yet we have nothing on Mahoney or his wife, I can't connect them to the crime."

"Well, maybe something will turn up," Martin said giving me a hug.

"Yeah well I've got about a million and one things to do today, the party starts in less than six hours maybe I can think of something."

After leaving Martin and Oliver's art gallery, Officer Diaz and I ran down to get the costumes for tonight. He was a good sport about it, helping me with getting everything into my tiny trunk and back seat of

my bug convertible. "So, Diaz, what did you do to get this babysitting job?"

"To tell you the truth, I volunteered for it." Mario Lopez's smile and all.

"Why?"

"I'm trying to get a promotion, you see my girlfriend Lindsey is having a birthday in a few days, and I'm taking her down to La Jolla beach, and I'm going to propose to her."

"Oh, that's so sweet, what a guy."

He pulled a black box from his front pocket and showed me the ring.

"Wow! This is beautiful."

The 1 1/2 karat round diamond solitaire in platinum sparkled before me.

"Yeah I hope she likes It," he said with a big smile on his face.

"I can see why you need this promotion now; you want a family right away?"

"Oh yeah, I can't wait, Lindsey and I have always wanted four kids, 2 boys and 2 girls, I come from a family of five and we had a blast growing up."

"I'm happy for you Officer Diaz."

"It's Jason, but all my friends call me Jay."

"Well, I'm happy for you Jay."

"Thanks," he put the black box back in his pocket. "What about you, ever think of getting married and having kids?"

"Well, I guess you could say I'm not quite there yet,"

I told him I'm still wondering where my feelings lie with Matt, and now that Detective Anderson was in the picture, well I like him too, and as far as marriage, I know I'm nowhere near that one.

"Don't worry you have plenty of time."

"Yeah, and according to Craig I even have people betting on which one I'll pick."

His tone softened and he said, "I didn't put any money on that bet, I thought it was pretty messed up."

"Thanks, Jay, I'm glad you're my shadow."

I put all of the costumes in my bedroom closet, went to the kitchen pulled out a Pierre kicked off my pumps, and rested on the patio lounge chair, only five hours to go. The countdown begins!

CHAPTER 19

It's Mardi Gras Time

By 6 pm, I had a long luxurious bubble bath with lavender oil, the sounds of Miles Davis on my I-phone, and my over- priced candles from Kiana's party. They were pretty and my bath is my oasis from all of the day-to-day excitement so I was ok with my purchase.

The women of Little Black Dress were ready to go to the DO NOT MISS, EVENT OF THE SUMMER! Our ball gowns so extreme and our faces of white powder, red lips, and 18-century hairstyles.
We looked like a time warp of the days of George Washington and Marie Antoinette, okay but not from the same country, she was from Austria, then she moved to France, and George well we all know that story.

We gathered together and took a bunch of pictures for our website, which would be up and running as soon as I could get someone to set it up. Computers, if you aren't on them, you're going to be left behind at least if you own a business.
The girls were all over the place, putting away makeup, closing duffle bags of clothes, putting on high heels, or trying to use the bathroom with these grand ball gowns on.

"Okay, girls is everyone ready?"

"Shoot I have a run in my hose, damn!" Roxy shouted

"Here I have extra." one of the girls said digging into her bright pink bag and looking for her spare pantyhose."

"Yeah, I'm not used to wearing these things either," I said pulling up my lace thigh highs.

We were ready to head out when my cell chimed Dave Brubeck's Take Five.

"Hello,"

"Hey Sunshine,"

"Detective Anderson, how are you?"

The girls whistled in the background and smiled, one of them even mimed a kiss. Roxy smacked her bottom and laughed, mouthing the words "Get it, girl."

I mouthed the words OMG and I went out to the patio to get some privacy from the noisy girl-filled living room of mine.

"You got a cheering section for me?"

"Oh yeah, sure, so tell me what do you want?" I asked him jokingly, of course.

"I just wanted to let you know that I had a long conversation with Matt about his past girlfriends. He gave me the names of a few women. I looked into them and found nothing."

"Then who is doing this?"

"Trust me I'm trying to find out. Did Matt ever talk about having any admirers or any women he saved from a fire? Sometimes people can fall in love with a person that rescues them from a tragic moment?"

"No, Matt never had anything like that, all the women he saved were thankful, one lady even bought a case of calendars, and gave them to her co-workers, but that was more like a thank you to the fire department. A lot of girls flirt with him all the time, maybe he flirted a little too much with one of them and they took it for something else. I don't know!"

"Okay if you can think of anything call me, I haven't given up, ok, Officer Diaz will be with you the whole time tonight, and I also have Summer being followed too. Have you received any more calls from the stalker?"

"No! All quiet on the western front here."

"That's exactly what I thought. I believe the stalker is waiting for the opportunity to strike, and I think tonight is it. I will be there tonight with an undercover team to surveil the area. The Mayor has his own security, and there will be a few uniformed officers at the event tonight, so you don't have to worry about being protected. I might be late, I'm checking out a lead."

I was now nervous as all hell, somebody out there wanted me and Summer dead, someone sick and diabolical, taunting us and following us. I was really scared now, and I just hoped Detective Anderson had enough officers to take care of this.

"Are you still there, Nikki?"

I guess I was silent longer than I thought, so I spoke up calmly and coolly. "Sure, I'm still here."

"Look, I know you're scared, but trust me, you'll be in a very public place with lots of people and cops, and I'll be watching you the whole time."

"I know, Paul, I'm just a little nervous."
I turned my neck side to side to escape the kink that was building right now and shook it off.

"I'm fine, Paul. Look, I have to go. I'll see you there."
"See you in a few hours."

After I hung up, I took a huge breath, released it, and focused on a positive thought. Breathe, you are strong, and you have plenty of police around you tonight. Just get a grip.
I told myself over and over...

We arrived on time, just as the sky turned burnt orange, with cobalt blue coming in from the mountains. The large house was fabulous, just as the party planners had promised. There were tall flags on each corner of the backyard flying high in colors of orange, purple, green, red, and fuchsia pink.

The buffet table looked enormous, with four stations of five eight-foot serpentine tables; it resembled a large snake enclosing the buffet. There was more food here than I had ever seen. Seafood stations with shrimp, clams, fresh Salmon and capers, and crab legs. Hors d' Oeuvres, of canapés, bacon-wrapped dates, hushpuppies, cheeses, relishes, olives from around the world, and grilled BBQ, ribs, chicken, brisket, and the wildest desserts, crème brûlée, cherries jubilee, bananas foster, fruits, kiwis, strawberry, pineapple, raspberries, and veggies, salads, gumbo, jambalaya. Two large ice sculptures, one of mermaids and one of a large saxophone, stood tall on the seafood table.

The three cakes had their own tables as well, they were spotlighted and draped with pink silky chiffon in the background of their tables. The pool had actual mermaids, no not really, just skinny women in shell bikini tops with sequined mermaid costumes swimming around.

They all had long hair wigs, in blond, brown, and red hair, their makeup of aqua and green glitter shadow, fake lashes, and heavy mascara highlighted their eyes, and bright red lip color completed the look, like a Vegas showgirl, they were actually pretty cool.

I whistled! "Pretty snazzy, don't you think, ladies?"

I asked the girls and Officer Diaz, all standing with their jaws on the floor.

"Pretty classy joint." Diaz concluded,

"Money talks." Roxy said,

"It's like Disneyland." I remarked,

"No Vegas, definitely." Roxy said.

We all nodded in agreement,

"Let's get to work, girls." I said going to the van to unload.

We warmed up with a few songs, testing mics, and sound. Officer Diaz stood off the side of the stage, his radio in his hand, checking in with the other fellow officers in plain clothes mingling about with the Mayor's security doing checks around the property.

A lighting guy dressed in a tux with his long blond ponytail came by. Diaz rushed by my side.

"Hey, I'm Mike Robbins, I'll be your lighting guy for the evening," he said, shaking my hand.

"Okay, I'm Nikki Rodriguez, my band Little Black Dress, and this is Officer Diaz." I said, introducing us,

"You guys from a prison?" Mike's eyebrows shot up!

"No, I have a stalker; it's a long story," I waved it off.

"Wow! Anyway, it's nice to meet you all."

"I have a little request, Mike."

"Oh yeah, shoot."

"No spotlight, please," I said with my hands together in a praying motion.

"The last gig we had, kept a spotlight on us forever, we were seeing spots for days," I said.

"That won't be a problem for you, the Mrs." He held up quotes with his fingers. "Only wants a spotlight for the announcements and happy birthday, she made it clear, only for the important events of the evening," he gruffed.

"It's nice to know we're not important." I replied,

" This brawd is lucky she's paying me a lot for this gig, I'm a professional, I do lighting for Taylor Swift, The Weekend, and Bruce Springsting, and I work with the biggest bands in the business."

He looked like his blood pressure was escalating; he pulled out a cigarette and lit up. He took a long swig of it and then blew it out away from us.

"Hey, Mike, don't worry about it. A gig is a gig, right,

you think my band likes dressing up like an 18th century Ho, c'mon now, ya with me."

He chuckled, "Yeah, at least I don't have to wear that shit." He took another long swig and extinguished his habit with his black cowboy boot.

"Thanks, Mike." I patted him on the back,

"All right, we're cool, Nikki."

He gave a thumbs-up and winked.

Mrs. Mahoney's Hench Tina, the lavender-suited lady who was her assistant, called out to Mike, her clipboard in her hands. He rolled his eyes.

"Not again, now what?"

"Think of the check, Mike."

He nodded in agreement. "It's a good thing I'm on my way to Hawaii after this one."

The clipboard lady walked up to Mike, scolding him,

"I made it very clear, Mr. Robbins, *NO* smoking!"

Mike went back to his work, clipboard lady went off to scold the catering staff.

I so need a vacation

We went back to rehearsal, touched up our faces, and started to play music as some of the guests began to arrive.

CHAPTER 20

Time to Party

We played for an hour or so and then earned a much-needed dinner break. The Dixie Land band relieved us for the next two hours. We all went our separate ways, bathroom breaks, water breaks, and of course, we were all anxious to try the food.

I held up one side of the dress so it would not drag on the floor when I walked. I headed for the buffet of Caribbean BBQ. Jerk chicken, Salmon, Scallops, pulled pork, what a great selection, it would be tuff but I went with the Salmon glazed in pineapple, and guava sauce.

"No Scallops tonight."

The familiar voice asked in my ear,

"Well, if it isn't Rhet Butler!"

Matt opened his suit jacket to show off his costume.

"It's a good look for me, huh?"

"Oh yeah."

"And you look beautiful as ever, Nikki. Good evening, Officer Diaz."

He tipped his hat to my shadow.

"Good evening, Matt," Diaz replied.

"So, where is Scarlet O' Hara?"

I went back to my side dish selections on the buffet, not really caring where Summer was, but just making conversation.

"She and Trixie are in the ladies' room, adjusting her costume."
He filled his plate with scallops and a large scoop of mashed potatoes.

"Trixie got an invitation, I'm shocked!"

"She volunteers as a youth counselor at the community center; anyone who works for the city was invited."
I had to admit he looked rather yummy as Clark Gable, very suitable.

"So, are you hungry?" I said, referring to his heaping plate of food. "We had a training exercise today. I'm starving."

"Well, don't give yourself an upset stomach."

"I won't, so where is your friend, Det. Anderson?"

"He's somewhere around here, although I haven't seen him yet."

"You didn't come together?"

"No, I came with the band,"
I said, reaching for a roll and butter.
We took our plates to a table with metallic green linens and metallic pink napkins.
Matt set down his plate and pulled out a chair for me.

"Look, I'll just sit here until your sweetheart comes, and then I'm out of here."

"It might be a while now, she's in line with Trixie at the buffet, she'll be there till next Tuesday," he looked annoyed.

Officer Diaz stood a few feet away from the table to give us privacy.

"Would you like anything from the bar?" Matt asked,

"Coke, please."

"I'll be right back," he left for the bar.

I had a few bites of the food, sheer heaven in my opinion. Between bites, I scanned the place for Paul. I wondered if he had any news yet. I pulled up my dress ever so slightly and fished my cell phone out of my garter belt. No messages, damn, where was he?

"Here you go, one Coke on the rocks." Matt placed my drink on the table.

"Thanks."

I took a long drink

"Slow down, girl, you part camel?" he smiled.

That smile that always gave me butterflies.

"It gets really hot on stage with all the lights, you know."

"I can see."

We were quiet for a few minutes just eating, and each one of us realized the silence was awkward, but did not know what to say.

It was strange, Matt and I were never so distant before, and it made me feel sad inside. I saw Miss Summer Simmons filling her plate with salad and fruit, not a carnivore like me, I take it. Matt would probably ask her to move in with him, and she would say yes, unlike me afraid of commitment. I finally admitted it to myself.

"What's wrong? Why do you look so sad?" Matt's hand on my cheek

"Oh, it's nothing."

"You could always tell me anything."

"I'm just nervous, that's all," I replied.

"Well, I think you're going to be fine, you have police protection, and if anyone wants to hurt you, they'll have to go through me too!"

For a moment there, we were suspended in time, like a dream, with no music and no other voices or sounds, just the two of us.
My eyes watered, so I dabbed at them with my napkin. Matt was close to me now.
"Don't cry, Nikki."
He spoke softly.
Our faces were very close now; his smell was clean and fresh with a light new leather smell.
"I'll be fine..."
His lips pressed against mine, soft, moist, warm...
We parted slowly, and my eyes opened,
"Matt I..."
I tried to say, but he spoke first,
"I'm sorry about that, it won't happen again."

"Oh, Matt don't ..." My cell rang out Take 5, it was Anderson.

"Hi, Paul."

"Hey, I've got news for you."

"About my case?"

"No, about Chanel."

"Matt, listen to this."

I turned up the volume on the phone, and Matt put his ear next to mine to hear Anderson.

"Matt's listening too, so what did you find out?"

"Hey, Matt"

"Anderson" Matt replied,

"So here it goes, I went back to Chanel O' Conner's condo, and I looked in that hiding space in the floorboard, where you found her journal. I thought maybe we missed something, so I checked it again, and guess what I found."

Matt and I were all ears now, both of us on the edge of our seats.

"What!" I asked,

"Yeah, what did you find?" Matt asked,

"I found two pictures of Mayor Mahoney and Chanel drinking Margaritas at the Hacienda Del La Fuente in Baja California,

I went there and showed the pictures to a few staff members there and they confirmed seeing them. The Manager said he rented a room to them, just one room that they both stayed in. And get this, they said they were newlyweds."

"What!" Matt and I said in unison,

"Yeah, that's right, confirming that he lied to us about his affair with her. I just got off a plane from Baja.

I should be there in twenty minutes. Look, I need to go, we're taking him in."

"I'll see you when you get here."

"Don't say a word to anyone," Paul said

I hung up the phone and put it back in my garter.
"Nice hiding place," Matt said. He took a long drink of what I presumed was a beer.

"I guess this is it."

"I guess so."

CHAPTER 21

Oh No

With just twenty more minutes of this dinner break, I decided to head to the ladies' room.

Summer and Trixie had just arrived at the table when I got up to leave.

"Leaving so soon, Nikki?" Summer asked

"Afraid so, I have to get back to the band."

"I guess you'd better go!" Trixie said in a foul manner,

"Enjoy your dinner." I said,

"Oh, Summer, do you know where the ladies' room is?" I asked,

"Just go past the stage, on the left side, there are cabanas marked ladies' room."

"Thanks."

I gave one last look at Matt.

He mouthed the words "I'll call you."

So Summer and Trixie wouldn't see

Officer Diaz, and I walked toward the cabanas.

We met up with Mrs. Green, who was walking from the cabanas.

"Nikki, you look lovely."

"Thank you, Mrs. Green and Marge," I said, rather thrown back

Mrs. Green and Marge were dressed in 1960s GOGO dancer costumes with bouffant flip-style hair do's and a full string of colorful Mardi Gras beads around their necks.

"You guys look great."

"Oh, we just pulled this stuff out of the mothballs," Marge replied. "Did you get a load of our dates?" Mrs. Green pointed to two tall Elvis impersonators.

"Fabulous, I didn't know you two were friends?"

"Oh, we go way back to our college days, we were roomies at Cal State Long Beach." Marge said,

"Well, you guys look so cool."

"Thanks," they said in unison

"Nikki, have you seen Martin and Oliver? They came as Roman warriors."

"Wow, hail Cesar,"

"I told them they looked groovy." The Elvis men came back to their dates,

"Girls, shall we go, we got a hunk-a hunk-a burning love."

Marge and Mrs. Green just laughed like schoolgirls and took the arm of their dates.

",Tootles" they said.

Diaz and I laughed,

"Cute," he said

"Aren't they?"

I went into the ladies' room cabana, Diaz checked the stalls, and then went back outside.

"You're clear," he said.

"Thanks,"

I was the only person in the cabana, which mainly consisted of a portable restroom, but in great style. The toilets were real, the sinks were porcelain, the counters were Corian, and the mirrors were large and full-length. The walls were painted in pale peach, and the stall doors were made from birch. The name of the company, "Tasteful Cabanas," left business cards on the counter of the vanity section. Wow, a full vanity complete with lotions, perfume, tissues, and mouthwash. Pretty fancy.

I got myself in the stall, did what I needed to do, and was out in a flash. I used the high-end lotion that sat on the counter and reapplied my lipstick. I put my compact purse, which was not bigger than a deck of cards, back in my garter on the other side from where I had my cell. "At least garters are good for something."

I got back to the stage and found the girls getting ready to go back on in a few minutes. We were behind the metallic Pink curtain, off to the side, waiting for the band ahead of us to collect their instruments. Clipboard lady came back in full force, looking haggard but still bitchy.

"Okay, I need your band to put your instruments in the storage shed," she directed the Dixie Land band to a cottage-style shed that looked like a large dollhouse.

Clipboard lady held up a pair of keys with a strange gold key chain. She walked over to the dollhouse, opened it, and waited impatiently for the band to follow.

When she came back to the stage, she motioned for me,

"Okay, now get this right when I signal you like this." She held out her right hand and made the thumbs-up signal.

"That means, stop your song and introduce me, this is what you're going to say."

She handed me a small piece of paper with her instructions.

"I will come up here on the stage, and I will introduce Mr. and Mrs. Mahoney. They will come up to the stage, and then we wheel out all of the cakes, and all the champagne glasses will be filled

before they get up to the stage." She was making more notes on her

clipboard. Her lopsided French twist had wisps of hair

sprouting out at different angles. Her brow with a gleam of sweat.

"I understand what I need to do." I told her,

"Good, then we're ready."

She held up her keys.

"Could you do me a favor and hand these keys to the Dixie Land Band? I have to run to the kitchen and make sure everything there is ready to

go."

"No problem, by the way, who do these keys belong to?" I asked,

looking at the key chain that seemed strange,

"Oh, those are Mrs. Mahoney's keys."

"I think you broke the key chain," I said, holding it up.

"Oh, don't worry about it. Mrs. Mahoney broke them last week when

she dropped them on the marble in the foyer."

"Is this a letter?"

"Yes, it was a letter M she was given the key chain last year, at the

Women of Rancho Niguel Conference she was the keynote speaker there, just one of the many contributions she is available for. Mrs. Mahoney mentioned we could count on you for political support. Can you donate a benefit concert, or do you want to stuff envelopes?"

"I uhh... A concert, I'll uh."

"Oh great, I'll put you down for singing at a benefit, obviously, there is no pay for that, as it's a donation. Well, thank you, and remember my signal."

Then she was off to the kitchen at lightning speed.

I couldn't believe she wrangled me into a free concert; the girls would not be happy about that one. I held up the keys and looked them over. They remind me of something, think Nikki. I couldn't place them yet, then I shrugged.

Whatever.

I handed them off to the Dixie Land Band, which I had to admit they were fantastic, all the way from New Orleans. One day, I would have to go there and experience a real Mardi Gras.

I went to the mic to start a song with the band.

The party was in full swing, the line at the buffet was still going strong, and the dance floor filled quickly, to my tune of "The Girl from Ipanema." The servers were going around and filling the glasses with Christol Champagne.

The gold bubbles filled their way to the tops of the flutes, crisp, fizzy. My Sax player came to her solo in the song, which always made the crowd go wild. For the next few seconds, I was hashing over the keys.

Something kept telling me it was all about the keys. Why was it familiar? As my mind turned all of the evidence over in my brain, the Piano solo came next.

Thinking and thinking and counting the beats of the piano and then smack!! Oh, that's it! I nearly yelled it out loud, but stopped myself and then sang as my part of the song came up. I sang my little heart out.

I saw the thumbs-up from clipboard lady. We finished our song, and I introduced her. She had straightened her French twist and applied a freshly painted face; she walked the stairs graciously, and I handed her the mic.

"Thank you, Miss Rodriguez, and let's have another hand for Little

Black Dress aren't they great?" she clapped.

The cheers were high and heavy, and we took our bows and stepped backstage.

I pulled up my dress, yanked out my cell, and dialed Anderson's number. Come on, pick up Paul.

It went to voicemail. I dialed it again, voicemail!

"Shoot!"

I paced back and forth, the introductions being made, and Mr. and Mrs. Mahoney were walking the line to the stage.

Where is Anderson?

"Are you okay, babe?" Roxy asked me,

"No, I need to get a hold of Detective Anderson."

"Why?" she asked me.

"Let me just say something big is going to go down, see if you can find him, tell him I need to talk to him."

With that, I spun on my heels and went out the back way off the stage.

I walked behind the cabanas, almost running, and I knew I had to find Anderson.

Swish, swish went my dress. I was really putting in overtime on this case, and I just hoped these shoes wouldn't give out on me.

The happy birthday had begun, and guests were holding up their glasses. I played back the details of the case over in my head.

Chanel O' Conner was killed by blunt force trauma to the head. She had smoke inhalation due to the fire that was caused by the candelabra that allegedly fell and started the fire. Smoke alarms with no batteries, a broken piece of a gold letter.

The murder weapon had to be something that was in the possession of the murderer.

I spotted the Dixie Land Band in the buffet line, striped red and white suit jackets on with white pants. I walked over to the lead singer, a man about in his 50s with grey hair and thick glasses that fell on his nose. I tapped him on the shoulder.

"Hi, excuse me."

"Well, hello," he said, turning to me.

"Hi, I'm Nikki Rodriguez from Little Black Dress."

"Oh yes, I know you have that lovely band, you play pretty good."

"Thank you." I was flattered,

"What can I do for your child?"

"I just need the keys to the shed. One of my band members forgot her cell phone in there. It fell out of her purse, she is going crazy over it, and her fiancé just bought it for her, so you can see I need to get it for her." I lied, but it was for a good cause.

"No problem, Nikki," he said, reaching into his coat pocket.

"Here you go, just return them when you're done, we go back on in 1/2 an hour."

"No problem, thanks," I said, bidding goodbye.

I ran to the side of the house where the wait staff had been going in and out of. It led to the kitchen and then to the long hallway where the study was.

I passed a few exhausted waiters taking a break, nibbling on cheese and fruit, and talking about the Dodger game they were watching on someone's cell phone.

I headed to the long hallway, creeping slowly without a sound. I took off my heels so I would be faster and quieter on my feet. Opening a few doors here and there, but nothing yet! I had to find one that led to the garage.

I heard a few whispers coming from the left. I ducked into a room. Closed the door and held my breath.

The many lights outside lit not only the massive patio but also some of the rooms in the house.

The shadows on the wall were those of a desk and a chair, bookshelves, and a large file cabinet.

A stroke of luck, it had to be Mrs. Mahoney's office, well, she had style, I'd give her that. The furniture was expensive, like the kind you see in the white house. I had no idea what it was called or what century it was from, but it was beautiful. Royal and expensive looking, I opened what looked like a closet door, nothing but a few blazers and some hangers. Ok, dig for clues, there has to be something here that I can use as proof.

213

I'm sure about now Officer Diaz was going ballistic searching for me, I was sorry to sneak away from him, but this was police biz, even though I'm not a cop.

I searched the desk, a calendar, and a notepad. Next, I opened the only drawer on the desk, empty. Doesn't she do any work here?
I tried the file cabinets, files of upcoming city events, and some campaign letters, but nothing. She must keep a laptop or something, but there was no trace of any devices here.
It was time to move on; nothing incriminating here.
I opened the door to the office just a crack to see if the coast was clear. When it was I sashayed down the hall in my big red dress, the long hall turned right, and just a few doors were here.

Great talk about the Winchester Mansion. Where does this place end?
I had luck on the third and final door.
Viola, the garage! The row of cars before me were all worth more than I'd ever made in my life.

A white Bentley fully loaded, of course, but then again, I don't know do they have a stripped-down model, who knows?
The next car was a European sports thing convertible, and it looked like fun.
A silver Jag lay next to it, and last but not least, a black Mercedes, SLK, E, or S, I don't know if they weren't in my price range, then I didn't have a clue. The thing I did know was that it was a dark sedan.

I looked around the car searching for scratches, and sure enough, on the right lower end of the front bumper, it was scraped, and some of the black paint was missing.

I opened up my cell phone and dialed Anderson's number, Come on, pick up, please pick up. I got a loud beep, beep. I looked at the screen of the phone, and it said no signal.
Crap, I slapped my forehead. Damn, these new homes, there is never a signal in these things. I got up from the floor and went to the trunk of the car. I put the keys in the lock and turned it.
It popped open, the light from the trunk giving me more light to search for clues.

There were some boxes of fliers, campaigning for Mr. Mahoney for Governor. An emergency kit in a leather bag, filled with band-aids, gauze, a flashlight, a solar radio, and other first aid stuff. Next to it was a linen pillowcase, with something in it.
Okay, so in movies, when the cops find evidence, they don't put their fingerprints on it; they usually have gloves or something to look through the stuff they find. Lucky for me, I had on my elbow-length red satin gloves. "Ok, be smart here." I was saying out loud.
I opened the pillow case and found clothes, a white suit with Ta-Da browned blood stains, yuck, I shoved the clothes back in the pillow case, and I pulled the case towards me, not realizing it would be so heavy.
"What the hell?" I opened the pillowcase again and took out the clothes, then looked into the bottom of the heavy case, and it was a Waterford crystal angel. The kind you see at Macy's that costs more than two gigs for me to buy.

215

At the time it was purchased, it was probably a beautiful, clear, precise cut crystal, with perfect lines and shape; now it was darkened with a deep brown-purple stain to it.

I had just found the murder weapon!

I thought of the blow this must have delivered, and it gave me chills to know this piece of glass had ended a life.

I need to get this to Anderson and fast. Where was he? I pulled out my cell, said a prayer, and tried to get a signal. There went that beep again, no service, damn!

I put the crystal angel back in the pillowcase, stunned by my suspicions of being dead on the right. Now all I had to do was get out of here alive, but that was going to be a problem.

"Drop it now or you're dead!"

I froze! Someone had followed me.

Chapter 22

It's You

A voice, one that I knew came from behind me.

I dropped the pillowcase and slowly turned around to face a black gun that was pointed at my head.

Lavender suit lady, AKA Tina or clipboard lady, take your pick.

She was all of the above, now she was here, holding me at gunpoint.

"Look, I just got lost, came into the garage, and the trunk was open, so I was just going to close it for you. You wouldn't want Mrs. Mahoney's battery to die now." I pretended to try to stall.

"Oh shut up, she never uses that car, I do, and you think I'm stupid, I know you're working with the cop."

She said, keeping her firm grip on the gun.

"Now put your hands up."

She yelled with more force.

I did as she told me and put my red-gloved hands in the air.

My cell phone fell into the trunk of the Mercedes, still roaming and searching for a possible signal. Now, how can I get out?

I was screwed!! Stuck in a garage with a psycho.

"You think you're so smart, little Miss Nancy Drew found a clue!" she smirked at me.

"Oh no, I'm no Nancy Drew, as I said, I was just walking by and...

"Oh shut up, I know you and your cop friend Detective Anderson are working together. I've seen the two of you having dinner, at Kendle's, and that other guy, the cute fireman, the one you're still in love with, come on, make up your mind already."

Was it that obvious? Am I as indecisive as that, a total stranger can see all of this?

"Look, it's complicated, I like both of them, I just, well, I'm just not ready to make a choice, and I'm not ready to settle down."

"Well, you're running out of time, sister. I've seen the other girl around your fireman, and you've got competition."

"You really think so?"

"Oh yeah, she's gorgeous."

"Thanks!" I said smart ass in my ways,

"What've you got to lose? The cop is a good catch, too!"

Wait a minute, what was going on here? I was having a conversation about my love life with a killer holding a gun to my head. I was at my worst, wasn't I?

"Did you kill Channel O'Connor?" I blurted out, still with my hands up in the air.

She gave that nasty smirk again,

"I had to. That little bitch was going to ruin everything I worked so hard for!"

"What do you mean?"

"What do I mean? I swear, everyone thinks I'm invisible. I worked my ass off at Harvard Law School, I got this job as Mrs. Mahoney's assistant, and I was going to follow them all the way to the White House.

My dream was clear: first the assistant, then the ladder to a position as a Secretary of Defense or an Aide to the President. I was on my way, my little ole southern belle ass in the White House, just a little gal from Tennessee, can you imagine."

Her southern accent had resurfaced, and now Annie get your gun had gone psycho path, with her passion for success turning into a passion for power. I had to be smart; maybe I could get her comfortable with me, and she could relax.

"Oh my God, Harvard, wow!" I embellished.

"Yeah, I was the first girl in my family to graduate with a college degree," she said with pride.

I looked down at my cell phone in the corner of the trunk.

"Tina, tell me why did you kill her if she was going to end the relationship?"

"She wasn't going to end it that whore, she had all of these late meetings with him, I knew what they were doing, I followed them."

She relaxed a little now as she walked back and forth in front of the trunk, but she was still holding the gun.

When her back was turned, I pushed the redial button on the cell and then put my hands back up.

"That Chanel and Mr. Mahoney, do you know what they were going to do?" she said, turning back to me.

I shook my head no.

"Well, I'll tell ya, they were going to go away and get married, he was going to divorce his wife and leave me." She walked back and forth again, her pacing no doubt was her frustration at the events that occurred.

"I couldn't have that! I worked too hard to get here. How could he do that? Didn't he know how close we are to the White House? He already has the Governor's spot in the bag." Her accent becoming thicker now. I took a peek at the phone, it had dialed Anderson's number and it was ringing, I spoke up to make interference so she wouldn't hear the dialing.

"So then how did you kill her?"

"Oh, it was easy, that ole boyfriend of hers, John Amos, paid her a visit, they argued, and then they ended up in bed together. She wasn't that over him, although he was kinda hot, you know, in a bad boy kinda way. When he left, I rang the doorbell, and she let me in. I tried to be nice to her, I told her to leave and be on her way, and I even offered her money. She told me to get the hell out and that she didn't need any money from me. I got really mad at her and said

"I'll give you one more chance to leave Mr. Mahoney and go on your way. When she laughed in my face, that was it... I got so stinking mad I gave her a slap, and then she slapped me back, we fought, like mad cats over a dumpster dinner.

Then I pushed her down, and she said I would be finished in the Mayor's office, she said I would never work in politics again, she was going to tell Grant, and that would be the end of me. I couldn't take any more, she just made me so Mad." She hit the air with her gun, punctuating the anger she had for Chanel.

"Then I realized she had to go, and then that's when I did it."

She was waving her gun around now; she hadn't noticed that I had put my hands down.

I heard a faint hello over the line on my cell, so I spoke up to clue in Anderson.

"What did you do, how did you finish Chanel O' Conner off!"

I said loud and clear, Anderson asked, "Where are you, Nikki?"

"Tell me, Tina, in this here garage at this party, how did you finish off that bitch."

I said, hoping to God, Paul heard me.

Her ego got the best of her, and now that she thought I had sympathy for her, she dove right in like an old gossiping girlfriend.

"I stood over that whore, and I grabbed the crystal angel that sat on the fireplace mantle, and I hit her over the head with it. She went down fast, and blood went everywhere."

221

She was saying as if she was looking back and seeing it again. "Then I lit the candles, and I took out the batteries from the fire alarms. I grabbed a steak knife from the kitchen and jammed the sprinklers. Last, I pushed over the candelabras, and I left as the curtains caught fire. My plan worked out so brilliantly. I had to cover my tracks. She had other evidence. She knew someone was following her. She thought it was the Mrs., but the Mrs. sure doesn't know what's going on."

"What about John Amos? He confessed to the crime and committed suicide!"

"Oh, that, I had the Sheriff of the county jail take care of him, you see the Sheriff runs a little money ring out of his jail, and I bargained with him to get rid of Amos, or I was going to the Mayor and the press with his dirty little secret.

"Did Amos know about the journal?" I asked her.

"No, I broke into Chanel's condo one night when she was writing in it, and I saw her put it in her large walk-in closet. I just didn't know where in the closet she put it. Then Mahoney paid her a visit, and I left and I ..." she stopped for a minute, psycho eyes darting back and forth as if she was making new calculations in her head.

"Wait, how did you know about the journal that wasn't in the papers?" Oh crap! I slipped up It was her at the condo looking for the journal that day I had hidden in the shower.
"It was you, the one who took the journal!"

222

Her eyes were wide and accusing

. She perked up and pointed the gun back at me.

"I have to get rid of you. Everything I told you, I have to kill you now, so sorry you won't be here to see us at the White House, Nikki Rodriguez!

She pulled a silencer from her coat pocket and put it on the gun. Come on, Paul, where are you? I searched for anything I could to protect myself, but not much would help stop a bullet.

"Goodbye, Ms. Rodriguez."

"Police drop your weapon," Paul screamed.

Coming through the garage door. Two other officers in SWAT gear joined him.

"You're surrounded by cops outside, too, so be smart and drop it!" Paul yelled again.

This time, Tina did what she was told and dropped her gun to the floor. Paul moved swiftly and kicked away the gun, then holstered his own weapon. Then he cuffed the killer.

The two SWAT officers kept a firm aim on her for any sudden movement.

"I want my lawyer." She yelled

Her arrogance was so annoying, she held her head up high and demanded to be given her phone call.

"You ok?" he asked me, touching my shoulder.

I caught my breath.

"Fine, here's all the evidence you need, plus she confessed everything to me."

I pointed to the stuff in the car.

223

"She'll be doing 20-to life," he said,

"Yeah, I'm just glad you came in time, otherwise you would have been investigating my murder."

"Thanks to your cell phone and the GPS tracking I bugged it with, I knew where you were."

"A bug! You put a bug in my cell phone? How did you do that? Is it legal?"

"Sunshine, you don't want to know!"

He put his arm around my shoulder and walked me out of the garage. Two other uniformed officers, plus Diaz, came into the garage now and took Tina, AKA Lavender suit lady, away for the murder of Chanel O'Conner.

CHAPTER 23

We have a Hero

I slept in really late, after the night I had, I deserved it.

It was 11:30 am Sunday morning, I rolled the covers off and hit the remote control, and turned on the TV. I hit XM satellite stations and piped in tunes from Count Basie. The trumpet music warmed my heart. Old school big band, what a way to wake up.

I showered and put on a nice little sundress with an orange, black, red, and green Hawaiian print.

I tossed my bouncy curls with finishing wax,

dotted on some makeup, put on my black strappy heels, and my Kate Spade bamboo purse.

Officer Diaz was right outside my door, waiting to chaperone me.

"Morning." I said,

"Good morning, Nikki."

"It's going to be a hot one today."

"I know"

I hopped in the red bug and put the top down to enjoy the sun and the warm 80-degree heat.

Starbucks was busy, with lots of people, clamoring about what was in the paper this morning, the scandal of the killer being caught.

"Jessica, it's busy today?" I said when I reached the counter,

"Oh my God!" She came out from behind the register and gave me a big hug.

"You're all right, oh thank God!"

"Yeah, I'm still here." I said,

"Everyone, it's her, this is the heroic Nikki Rodriguez."

Jessica said, bouncing around.

The crowd gave me a round of applause.

"What's going on, Jessica?"

"Nikki, you're famous, look!"

She ran to the newspaper holder and grabbed a copy of the Rancho Niguel Courier.

The picture of Tina being put into a police car, the headline read "Local Singer Nabs killer!"

Detective Paul Anderson was very happy to arrest Tina Highline, an assistant of Mrs. Grant Mahoney, last night during the lavish birthday party of Mayor Grant Mahoney at his home.

Detective Anderson credits Ms. Nikki Rodriguez, a lead singer for the band Little Black Dress located here in Rancho Niguel, for her bravery during the time she was a hostage held at gunpoint by Tina Highline.

"Ms. Rodriguez was a tremendous help on this case. She served as a witness and gave us a lead on the case that cracked it open."

Anderson went on to say that if it wasn't for the patience and quick thinking of Ms. Rodriguez, she wouldn't be here today.

"Ms. Rodriguez is a valuable asset to this community. The department thanks her for her help on this case."

Further, thanks came from Mr. & Mrs. Mahoney. *"She will be receiving the key to the city for her brave and heroic act for the city of Rancho Niguel. We are pleased to have a fine citizen like Ms. Rodriguez."* Obviously, there was no mention of the affair between Mahoney and Chanel; all of that was under the rug, so to speak.

I was glowing inside. After I finished the article, Jessica stood before me with my grande skinny vanilla latte.

"Isn't it great, Nikki, you're a hero?"

"I guess so."

"So, tell me, was it really scary? What happened? I want all the details, but later I have to get back to work."

"Okay, tomorrow," I said, heading out.

People in Starbucks shook my hand and waved to me when I left.

I walked over to my bug. I was a little star-struck by all of the attention I was given. A friendly face greeted me.

"Hey, what are you doing here?"

"I saw your car and thought I'd stop to say hi, and I saw the paper this morning."

"Yeah, what a night, I think my adrenaline was going so fast that I didn't have time to think."

"I'm just glad you're all in one piece."

He came closer and put his arms around me.

He was intoxicating as he always was to me, giving me butterflies from his very closeness.

Still holding my latte, I put my arms around him.

Take 5 chimed along loud and clear.

We parted, and I put my latte on the hood and searched my purse for my cell.

"Hello, detective."

Matt moved back a foot, hands on his hips, waiting patiently

"Hello Sunshine, did you see the papers this morning? You're a hero."

"I did thank you."

"I also have it on good word that the FBI is arresting the Sheriff who's involved in a money/drug ring. So I thank you for all of the crimes we have been able to solve, and I just want you to know I'm taking you out for a celebration tonight. I will not take no for an answer."

I looked at Matt, and he was so patient, just waiting, giving me space, not knowing what Paul was saying.

"Nikki, are you still there?"

"Yeah, I'm here, umm, okay."

"I'll be at your place by 6 pm then." "All right."

"See you then."

"Bye,"

"Detective Anderson, huh?" he asked.

"Yeah,"

"So you have a date tonight."

"Yes, oh Matt, do I detect jealousy?"

"Not at all."

"Let's sit and talk on the patio."

"Okay, sure."

Matt went in to get his Venti iced mocha, and I selected the plush patio couch by the fire pit.

Matt was out after a few minutes, beaming,

"It seems like you have a fan club in there."

"A fan club already, wow."

"Everybody loves a hero."

"Isn't it the truth, so what's on your mind?" I asked him,

"Last night at the party, when I kissed you."

Here it comes, I knew we would need to talk about that kiss and what it really meant.

"I've come to a decision about us," he said, choosing his words carefully.

"Matt, before you say anything, I just want you to know I want to keep our friendship." I told him,

"I'm breaking up with Summer." he said it as if it was something he needed to say.

"Oh, I didn't see that coming," I told him.

"I'm on my way to see her, right after this; it's just not working out with us."

This was something I didn't expect to hear from him. Miss Perfect wasn't perfect enough for him. What was with Matt?

"Why?" I asked him, not showing any hint of excitement.

"Because after that kiss, I realized I'm still not over you."

CHAPTER 24

A New Place

I may have gasped when he said that, I'm not sure, maybe he just caught me off guard since I had been reeling in the sudden swarm of attention that the community had bestowed on me. After what he said, we really didn't say much more.

Matt went off to see Summer and, as he put it, break it off gently. I decided I needed to get my mind off of everything; there was too much, and I needed to talk to my best friend. I dialed fast.

"Roxy here."

"Hey, chicky, we need a spa day."

"Ok, how about mañana" (meaning tomorrow in Spanish).

"Yes, Roxy, I have to get all of this figured out."

"I know after last night, oh my God. Unbelievable girlfriend, I am the best friend of a hero."

"Oh, that, yeah, but I need to sort out my love life."

"Ok, but let's go to breakfast first, we'll go to Laguna."

"That sounds wonderful."

"All right, babe, see you then at 9 am."

"Sounds good."

I was just putting my cell away when it chimed, take 5.

"Hello."

"Nikki, this is Oliver. Thank God you're all right, and we were so worried about you. When everything went down, the cops wouldn't let anyone near you. I just figured we'd catch up later, so tell me, how are you holding up?"

After my conversation with Oliver, I left the patio at Starbucks. I wanted to head out to Laguna right this minute, but getting away was not in the cards. I had a date later, and just when things couldn't get more complicated, Matt called me and said he needed to see me in a few hours to meet at my condo.

I went back home, did some light house cleaning, put in some laundry, and waited for him.

He arrived full of excitement and said he was taking me somewhere! Of course, I was clueless as to where we were going.

We drove up Water Creek Rd, heading north, going towards a posh neighborhood of two-story homes and green grassy lawns.

We pulled into the driveway of a two-story Spanish-style home. It was very nice; a cobblestone path with a border of tulips led up to a double door entrance of wood doors with iron hinges.

Matt took a gold key from his pocket and opened the doors.

We walked into bamboo hardwood floors and white walls. The home was empty but large and spacious.

"So what are we doing here, Matt?"

"I wanted you to be the first to see this. I just bought this house last month."

"What! You did, oh my God, congratulations, Matt." I hugged him, and he spun me around in his arms.

"Isn't it great?" he said with excitement.

"It's beautiful, but can you afford this?"

"Well, that's part of my good news, see with Tanks and Brinks retiring and the Captain getting his transfer to another house, there was a spot open for a new captain and yours truly got the job."

"You did, oh Matt, that's wonderful, when did you find out?"
We were all smiles and hugs now.
"Two months ago, I got the news, with a significant salary raise, and I was here in this area on a call, and the house just caught my attention, and it had a big for sale sign on it, so I called the realtor, saw the house, and I knew it was perfect. The owners wanted a fast sale, a quick escrow, and it was done.

I just got the keys about an hour ago."

"Oh, I'm so happy for you, Matt, that's really great."

"You have to come and see the pool out back," he said, grabbing me by the hand like a happy 10-year-old.

The yard was large with a full-size pool and spa, and an outdoor kitchen complete with a fire pit.
The yard extended to a grass area beyond the pool with a few lemon and orange trees to provide some shade for those summer days. "So when is the housewarming party?"

"After I get the house furnished, I'll have a big party."

"So let me see the rest of it."

"It's nice, it has four bedrooms and a game room/sports room, and it has a three-car garage."

"For your man cave." I laughed, typical guy, a sports room, they are all the same.

"Are you going to put a keg in there?"

"I thought about a nice classy bar, yeah, I have a lot of ideas."
We went upstairs to see the rooms.
Three good-sized guest rooms or offices, a guest bath with a full tub and the game/sports area, and a large bonus loft that looked out to the first floor. "Now this is the master bedroom."

He opened two double doors to a large room with white carpet, a balcony that viewed the pool and the mountains in the background, and a fireplace that was shared between the master bath and the bedroom. The high ceilings and windows made the room look enormous.
I walked into the master bath and was now very jealous.
A very large claw-foot tub sat in front of a huge oval window with the same view as the balcony, double sinks, and a separate vanity, a huge walk-in closet, a private room for the commode, and, of course, a large tiled shower with two shower heads with massage selections.

"Matt, I'm jealous, the tub is amazing."

"I knew you would like that, it has your name written all over it."

"You know me so well, wow, you bought a winner here."

"I thought so too."

"So what are you going to do with all this room?" I asked as I slipped off my shoes and climbed into the tub just to see what it would feel like. Bathtub heaven.

I snuggled in low and rested my head on the back of the tub; this thing was large enough to sleep in.

"I look at it as an investment, for the future," he had kneeled down now at the tub level.

I closed my eyes and said. "This is too comfortable,"

"I know," Matt said

"Maybe I should sell my condo and buy one of these."

"Maybe you should." he stood up and helped me out of that beautiful tub.

"Are you hungry?"

"Yes."

"Good, because I brought lunch."

We went back downstairs and out on the patio.

Matt went back to his truck and brought back a basket with lunch. We sat under the fruit trees on a plaid blanket and feasted on wine, pasta salad, roast beef sandwiches, and chocolate cake.

We reminisced and laughed about old times, work, and gigs, and there was no pressure, no romance, and no commitment; we were just two friends having lunch under some fruit trees.

Matt dropped me off at the condo around 5:30 pm.

"I'll see ya," he said,

"Ok bye."

I waved as he drove off, and went in to get ready for my date.

I got dolled up in a pair of black slacks and a silk off-the-shoulder top in turquoise. I let my long, brown curly locks run free tonight and put on dramatic eye makeup and mascara.

My cell rang again.

"Hi, are you on your way over?" I asked,

"Yeah, sorry I'm running late, but I think I have a lead on your

case. I did more digging, and you'll never guess who your stalker is..."

Everything went black! The room disappeared, and I fell to the floor! When I came too, I saw a blur of red hair and a figure standing over me. "Nikki, wake up."

My eyes focused, and now before me stood Trixie

"Trixie?" I said in a small voice,

"Yes, it's me, in the flesh."

"What are you doing here?"

I tried to get up, but then I noticed my hands were tied up, and she pointed a gun at me.

"What happened?" I asked,

"You passed out from the chloroform I gave you."

"Why are you doing this, Trixie?"

"Because you won't stay away from Matt!" she shouted,

"Ok, I know you're friends with Summer, but don't you think she can handle her own love life? I don't think she needs you to protect her."

"I'm not protecting her interest, I'm protecting mine." Her face contorted with anger.

It hit me, Trixie was my stalker! She was the one with the threatening messages. She worked in the city building, and she had access to the public phones as well. Why didn't I catch this? Some investigator I am!

"It's you!" I blurted out.

She put her gloved hands on her hips and tsk'd!

"For someone who solved a murder, it took you a while, yes, it was me, I set my sights on Matt, he would have been mine if Summer hadn't snatched him up, and then you kept coming back into the picture. I had to keep both of you away from him.

He broke up with Summer this morning. Poor thing was heartbroken, Matt was free, and I thought my prayers were answered. Until I followed him and saw him with you."

"No, it's not what you think, Trixie." I pleaded,

"Oh shut up, do you think I'm stupid?"

She was angry, now yelling and ranting about pacing without patience, in the living room.

Then her voice softened with insult.

"It's your fault, Nikki. Why couldn't you just stick with Det. Anderson he would be better for you. Just think of it, the two of you would solve cases together and be heroes in the city; it would have been great. He likes you. I've seen the way he looks at you. Gee, he's fallen hard for that one. Then Matt would have come to ME, but you're so selfish, and now I can't let you get in the way.

Matt and I will be together in that beautiful new house of his, we'll be married, and I'll have his children, we'll be fabulously happy."

"Trixie, does he know how you feel?"

"Not yet, but that's because you bitches have been in the way of him showing his true feelings for me."

"You haven't even dated him yet."

"Totally not my fault, Nikki, but I know Matt loves me, he comes in twice a week for groceries and always smiles at me and comes to my counter to order his turkey sandwich," she smiled.
This girl was nuts; she had this fantasy in her mind that Matt came by to see her, delusional, not just psycho.
I had to diffuse this one and fast. What was it with my luck, two psychos in one week?

"It's too late, I just have to get rid of you."

She opened a black bag that was sitting on the coffee table and pulled out a bottle of pills and a notepad.

"Here start writing."

She handed me the pad and a pen.

"What is this?" I asked,

"Your suicide note, see after Summer came here to tell you she and Matt were getting married, you went ballistic and killed her, then you couldn't take the pressure, and you killed yourself."

I laughed,

"Do you think anyone will believe that?"

"Of course they will, everyone knows you're still hung up on Matt."

She had it all planned out, walking about the room, her innocent red ponytail bobbing up and down.

"I'm not writing a suicide note for you, and besides, there is a cop outside. You'll never get away with this."

"Oh, you mean Officer Diaz, after I used my cat in tree act, he was putty in my hands, but don't worry, he won't be here to save you," she said innocently.

"What did you do to him?" I spat out

"I wouldn't worry about him, I'd be worried about my own pretty little head, now start writing!" she yelled and slammed the pen down on the coffee table.

Then she paced the living room and put her gun down next to some pictures on the mantel, with Matt and me.

A camping picture from our stay in Big Bear, there we are on skis on a white snowcapped mountain.

Another picture of us at a vineyard in Napa, under some trees. There was also one of the band members at a charity event sitting on the fire truck. She picked up one of them and flung it across the room, where it shattered. "He won't need any pictures of you in our new place. It's too bad you won't be at the wedding, it will be beautiful."

She walked about the living room like walking on a red carpet, her moods were strangely odd, up, down, frowning, smiling. I was getting vertigo from her personality.

"It's time to write the letter. Here's what I want you to say.

Dear Matt, I'm so sorry I had to do this, but I had no choice. My love for you was too much, and I had to get rid of Summer Simmons. She was in my way of getting you back. I'm sorry for all of this. One day, maybe you can forgive me.

Love
Nikki Rodriguez"

I wrote what she told me, the whole time looking for a way to get out. I had to think fast, but she was moving around so much I couldn't lock down one area of the condo to get out or get her out of the way.

I knew Paul was on his way, especially after my cell went dead. Where was he?

I had to stall until he arrived.

"So what are you going to do next?" I asked, hoping to get her to embellish and give me more time. She looked at me carefully, thinking through her next words.

She looked dreamily up at the ceiling fan and said,

"Matt will be so distraught after his ex-girlfriend killed his current girlfriend, and I will be there to comfort him." She was smiling at her vision of reality, which no doubt made me think her sanity was definitely on a crazy high. Her mood then shifted as if her patience had casually run thin, and she blurted out,

"Now sign the note and give me the pen."

She walked back to me without the gun, for some reason, she had let her guard down and became sloppy.

I had about a two-second window right about now; it was this or death. Slowly, the seconds or therefore second ticked like a stopwatch,

varying my decision, should I or shouldn't I, how much of a chance do I have? Do I hit her, push her, or just go for the total tackle like a linebacker?

"Here!" I said, pushing the paper forward with my tied hands, she was standing right beside me now, reading what I had written. I thought of jamming my pen in her stomach, but I wasn't sure that I could reach up high enough to hit any vital organs or tissue. The only other weapon I had was my head, so then I stood up as fast, and with all of the strength I could possibly put forth, I head-butted her. Pain vibrated from my forehead to the back of my neck, but I prevailed!

She lost her balance from the blow, and then I used my shoulder and pushed her into the wall, where she fell to the floor and passed out. I ran as fast as I could to get the gun on the mantel when the front door broke open with Detective Anderson coming in with the Cavalry.

Their guns drawn, they secured the room.

Trixie lay in a heap, still out cold on the floor. They cuffed her and took her out.

"You're late," I said, looking at Paul.

"Better late than never."

Anderson cut my ropes loose with his Swiss Army knife on his key chain. "This is twice in one week, sunshine. Do you need a permanent bodyguard?"

I was breathing heavily with exhaustion

"I'm just glad to see you."

"Me too." he hugged me.

Once again, the police sirens and the ambulance brought the whole complex out again, and all my neighbors were whispering and looking on as all the brouhaha was once again deployed.

Paul helped me to the back of an ambulance, his worried expression removed, and his calm and cool manner returned.

241

"How is Detective Diaz? I asked.

The EMT took my blood pressure and then started cleaning my rope burns.

"He's going to make it. Trixie shot him in the chest, but his vest saved his life; he'll make a full recovery."

"Oh, thank God." I breathed a sigh of relief.

"As for Summer, that's a different story."

The EMT finished his work.

"Thanks," I told him.

When we were alone, Paul sat next to me with his arm around me, my head on his shoulder.

"What happened?" I asked, full of shock.

"She was shot, a blow to the heart. We found her in the trunk of Trixie's car."

Tears came to my eyes, poor Summer, the thought of her trusting Trixie and never realizing the lie she was living with, how tragic it must have been to be deceived like that.

To think my body could have been stuffed in the trunk with Summer.

"How did you know Trixie was behind all of this?"

"I had the phones tapped in city hall, and when they went to your line, I had a time frame, and I coordinated it with the cameras in the city hall and nailed her right on camera. I was at her house when I called you, and then when your line went dead, I knew where she was." Martin and Oliver called out to me.

"Nikki,"

"Can you let them through?" I asked Paul.

He waved to the officer standing at the barricade to allow them to come in.

"Oh, Nikki, we were so worried about you." They hugged me.

"Such a tragedy." Oliver strained through his tears,

"Nikki, you could have been killed again!"

Martin shuddered at the thought.

Matt came running from the crowd towards me.

"Nikki,"

He embraced me tightly in his arms.

I looked him in the eyes.

"I'm sorry about Summer; she was a sweet person who didn't deserve this."

"It's my fault," he said with sadness and feeling responsible.

"Matt Trixie was obsessed. We found photos of you all over her room and love letters, and she even had wedding invitations printed with your name on them." Paul told us,

"My God, I never realized." Matt responded

"She wanted me to take the fall for killing Summer; she made me write a suicide note accompanied by pills to make it look like I killed myself."

"She looked so innocent, so normal, who would have guessed she was bad news?" Martin replied

"You never know," I said.

Paul went on, "No, it turns out Trixie AKA Sheila Dobbs has a history of this kind of behavior. She's wanted in connection with a Boston murder of a friend of hers, and she also has a warrant for a harassment and attempted murder charge from an incident with a girl who used to date her ex-boyfriend. Apparently, she tried to force this girl off a 50-foot bridge."

We were all stunned by Trixie's past. What a mess she was, and now she had really hurt someone to the point of murder. We were all quiet, just taking in the info from Paul and wondering why none of us had ever once thought of this girl as a troubled person who would push herself to such extreme behavior.

"Detective Anderson, the coroner needs to speak with you," a young officer said to Paul, breaking our silence.

"I'll be right back." He looked over at me.

Martin and Oliver stepped back and said their goodbyes.

"We're heading home, we'll call you tomorrow, Nikki." Martin said,

"Bye, Nikki." Oliver waved. Still sad with red-rimmed eyes.

"What a day, I'm just glad this is all over," Matt said, helping me out of the EMT van. "You have no idea how glad I am."

I stood up, folding the blue blanket that had been wrapped around my shoulders.

"How about a rain check on that dinner?" Paul asked when he walked back over to us.

"I'll be back at your place," Matt said, giving Paul and me a chance to talk.

"He really is feeling bad about Trixie, isn't he?"

"He feels bad he couldn't help Summer, and honestly, all I want to do is get back in bed and pull the covers over my head." I confessed,

"I don't blame you, I don't think I'd want to leave my place for a while, too, after what you've been through. I have a lot of work to take care of, but how about I bring us a midnight snack?" he smiled.

"That sounds good, better than calling me tomorrow."

He kissed me and drove off in his police cruiser.

CHAPTER 25

Matt's Housewarming Party

I made the papers again, the story was front-page news Monday morning about the psycho Trixie and her obsession with Matt. Summer's murder and the attempt on my life were all written in black and white.

The DA made their plea for 20 years in prison, but Trixie's lawyers wanted a deal for a state asylum so that she could get the help she needed, plus she was going to be extradited to Boston to face other charges for those crimes. The second article plastered on the front page read: The Sheriff of the county jail was arrested for a money/drug ring; agents busted this case after two months of an undercover sting.

Paul had stayed over last night after our midnight snack of nachos and fiesta tacos from Tia's Taco House.

"I'm sorry this was the only place open this late," he said at the door when I opened it."

"You're forgiven, come on in."

"I owe you a fancy dinner in Laguna, after a day of surfing, maybe."

"Ok, sounds good."

We ate, we had a few beers, and we fell asleep in our clothes on the living room sofas...

The next morning, he headed out early for a two-week mandatory training seminar.

"Two weeks in Santa Barbara, poor baby, I feel so sorry for you."
I teased him.

"It will be without seeing you."

We kissed and held each other close. "Will you be lonely without me?"

"Yes, but I do have work and some social engagements to attend.

Matt's housewarming party next week, for one thing, and then there's the retirement party for Tank and Brinks. We need to select music and start practicing for the event, it's set for late October, but we are still always prepared."

I sighed, taking a breath.

"When I come back, we'll hit the waves, ok."

"Sounds good, Kahuna."

After he left, I got showered and called my best pal, Roxy, to join me for breakfast at my house. I didn't have the strength to go out to Laguna today.

I made a nice Italian roast coffee in the French press for Roxy and me. Along with a bacon and veggie omelet that we took to the patio table. At this point, I needed my best friend's companionship, my shoulder to vent on. "The morning paper is filled with the news of Mayor Mahoney running for Governor of the state of California." Roxy blabbed on

"Yeah, well, it looks like he is making his play for the future, the White House, as Tina put it before she tried to kill me."

"Oh, he will probably do it, that's how they all get there, scandals and secrets."

"You forgot payouts!" "That too, I almost forgot."

"Roxy, look at it this way, Little Black Dress is booked until February 14, with work. Very good for our bank account." "Cheers to that." We clinked our coffee cups.
"Do you have the funnies?"

"Right here, darling" (it sounded more like d-aw-ling with an accent.)
"So what's the story with your love life, girly?"

"It's complicated." I sighed.

She switched gears and chatted about the upcoming events. "Matt's party is in two weeks, and the pancake breakfast and auction on Saturday morning." She winked, and I rolled my eyes, telling her I'm getting her hint at discussing my friendship with Matt.

"By the way, I'm bringing a new guy, he owns a tattoo parlor, and he says I should really start to ink up. I told him I only have two very small tats that he might have the privilege to see."
She smiled, giving me the lowdown

"Fun." I nodded,

"So, Nikki, are you taking Paul to Matt's party?"

"No, he's still going to be out of town in Santa Barbara; he's staying a few extra days to follow up on a case down there."

"Cool, that man is always solving cases, so are you guys keeping it cool or getting serious?"

"No strings, no complications, right?"

"Amen, sister." We clinked our coffee cups again.

After breakfast, we had a day of much-needed manicures and pedicures. Roxy and I went shopping and had lunch at Clara's Pizza Pie, for a large pepperoni with olives and extra cheese. Plus, we needed to catch up on our gossip. It was an all-out girls' day.

Two weeks later, Saturday morning rolled around quite fast. After a few long telephone calls to Paul during the week, we caught up on getting to know each other. I hadn't seen Matt for the past two in a half weeks. I had run into Tank, and he told me Matt was busy. Hmm, what was he up to?

I dressed in a short Black Country dress adorned with orange flowers on it, I pulled on a pair of cowgirl boots, and some turquoise jewelry to finish the look.

My long hair I left down with curls at the ends.

The morning was warm, not too cold or too hot, a nice 74 degrees.

I arrived at Rancho Niguel Park at 8 am, and already there were many families and kids coming with big appetites. The white tents and easy-ups, all lined in a nice and neat row, along the small pond that was in the center of the park.

The firemen, all clad in their navy blues, were one by one creating an assembly line for the distribution of lots of pancakes.

Children holding their white paper plates patiently waiting in line, their little mouths watering at the sight of hot pancakes with butter and syrup dripping over them. A hot grill with sausage cooking made the air smell of smoky mesquite.

A large white tent in the center of the park had all of the items that were being held for the silent auction.

I made a beeline to see the items I wanted to bid on.

I knew what I was looking for, the item I had been salivating to have, the Killer Cool Jazz painting.

It was going to go in my living room, right above the mantel. How beautiful it would look, a high-priced piece of art on my wall, in my home.

I walked into the tent, a light breeze accompanying me and giving me refuge from the already high sun. Long tables with white linens showcased some of the items up for auction. A large tin basin with t-shirts, caps, and a blanket, two tickets to the Angels baseball game VIP box suite. There was a

Picnic basket filled with pasta, cookware, and a $500 gift card to Olive Garden. The one from William Sonoma caught my eye, it was filled with a Kitchen Aid mixer in lemon yellow with a pack of white and pale green striped towels, red silicon spatulas, cake mix, and odds and ends for making goodies. Next, a year's worth of oil changes and car washes from Speedy Wash and Oil.

Sports-themed baskets with jerseys and coolers, BBQs with all of the trimmings like BBQ sauces from around the world. Picnic baskets filled with melamine dishes and plastic wine glasses, and adorned with expensive bottles of wine and cheese.

A large red Radio Flyer wagon filled with toddler toys and a few handbags from Michael Kors and Coach filled with sunglasses and wallets. There were lots of goods donated by restaurants, business services, free lawn maintenance for a year, free plumbing service, Hair salons, makeup companies, toy stores, and the baskets were great. I moved on to the pegboard they used to display the art, and right before my eyes, there it was, my painting.

"It's beautiful, isn't it, Nikki?" Martin said from behind me,

"Yes, it is, and it's going to be mine."

"Hi Nikki"

I turned to see Matt in his blue uniform holding a plate of pancakes. "Hi Matt,"

"These are for you." he handed me the plate.

"Thank you, you didn't have to do that."

"It's no problem."

"Nikki was just admiring this piece. I think she's going to go home with it," Martin said, jumping into the conversation.

"I saw this, and I thought of you. How did I know?" Matt smiled

"Well, as long as no one else outbids me," I replied

I ate my breakfast as we walked around the tables, talking and admiring the auction pieces.

Martin had excused himself to go and answer some questions for the gallery.

"So are you coming to the party tonight?"

"I'll be there, so have you gotten all the furniture for your house in already?

"Yeah, I've been busy the last two weeks, but everything looks good now." An announcement was made over the mic that they were going to start the bidding.

"Let's go grab a seat."

We walked over to the next tent to seats that were lined up in rows of 10. The auctioneer stood at a podium, mic in hand, he started in with typical auction jumbo,

"Hey folks, here we have a nice blown glass lawn ornament." He said in a booming, fast-paced voice.

A Vanna-type young girl modeled the glass, showing it from different angles, and then they started the bidding. "Do I have 100 now? 1 ok now 200 her over there 3 4 5." and so on, but much faster. "Sold!" The announcer roared.

After 20 minutes of fine vases and one collector car from a famous celebrity with a very large collection, my picture came up on the block.

The announcer said, "Folks, here we have a very nice painting, a local artist is an up-and-coming star in the art world, and this will be worth a fortune in years to come. This one, folks, is called Killer Cool Jazz, folks. Let's start the bidding at 500, do I have five?"

I raised my paddle.

Little lady there.

Yes, I have 6. ok, do I have 7?

I raised my paddle.

I have 8, ok, do I have 9?

I raised my paddle again.

My limit was 1500, and I knew I couldn't go higher than that.

From 1000, it was me and someone else. I craned my neck, but I couldn't see who was bidding against me. Finally, it was at 1500 my final bid,

"And going once, going twice, sold to the lady up front!"

I got it, Matt and I were hugging each other, I was so happy...

I bought the painting that I wanted. Clapping ensued, and my smile was as wide as the road.

I hung my new painting above the fireplace, and it fit perfectly.

After the auction, I came right home to put it up. My walls had been so boring, but now there was something festive and colorful to see. I just stood there admiring it for what seemed like hours, but it was only five minutes.

My day was going well, it was about 1:30 pm in the afternoon so I walked out to the corridor of mailboxes to see what junk mail awaited me.

It was a nice, warm 82 degrees outside, with pillow clouds and blue skies. "Hi, Nikki."

"Hello, Mrs. Green, off to work," she said in yellow scrubs with Disney princesses on them.

"Yes, one more day and I'm outta here for two weeks' vacation, Marge and I and the Elvises are going on a cruise to the Mexican Riviera." She did a little salsa dance move and hummed a tune.

Ahh, a vacation, it must be nice, I thought.

"Have fun, Mrs. Green." She really needs some time off.

"I will, dear, trust me, I need it, tootles."

She waved off

My cell chimed Take 5

"Mrs. Rodriguez hello, I'm, Judy with the Firemen's

Retirement Association for Rancho Niguel, and I'm calling to confirm Little Black Dress as the band for the retirement Party of Lieutenant Tank and Lieutenant Brinks in two weeks on October 30, since it's so close to Halloween we are making this a costume party theme. Your band can come dressed as anything you like." The retirement party, I couldn't wait for that. The band had begun practicing songs from the late 70s and early 80s, and we were so into it.

"Yes, I'm confirming we will be there."

"Okay, I will send out an itinerary and payment in full,

with all of the details, Ms. Rodriguez. Thank you."

"You're welcome bye." Wow, another costume party, well at least we

wouldn't look like hookers from the 1700s.

I hung up my cell.

I opened my box, junk mail, offers for credit cards, a water bill, an electric bill, and an invitation. I opened the Ivory envelope and pulled out an invitation of fine linen with calligraphy writing, the wedding of Officer Diaz.

An invitation to the wedding of

Detective Jason Diaz and Ms. Lindsey Smith request the honor of your presence at their wedding on the Eighteenth of December two thousand and twenty at 2:00 PM,

St. Mark's Catholic Church,

1215 Palm Drive,

Rancho Niguel, California 90340

The reception card read

The Huntington Hotel at Rancho Niguel

118 East Huntington Ave,
4 pm - 12 am
The R.S.V.P. Ms. Nikki Rodriguez and Guest

"So you're going to Diaz's wedding?" Craig asked over my shoulder, the stagnant smell of beef jerky lingering from him. He was dressed in khakis today and a white polo shirt. Pretty spiffy for him, not his usual gym attire.

"Of course, what about you?"

"Hell yeah, Nikki, I hear they're serving Prime rib, and word is they moved the wedding up because his girlfriend is preggers! Ha, it was supposed to be a Valentine's Day wedding, but she don't want to look fat for the pictures or something like that."

I ignored his food comment and his belittling gossip about Officer Diaz and his fiancé, Lindsey, so I inquired of Kiana instead.
"So how is the candle business going for Kiana?"
"She's doing really well, and thanks, Nikki, for helping her out. She appreciated your order."

This was a new Craig. Thanking me for something. Wait, something's up! My intuition was telling me he was gearing up for another favor.

"She's expecting your call for a party at your place."

"What!" I replied with complete shock and anger on my face.

"Yeah, Sunday 7ish, you know, just about ten people, drinks, and some light hors D'overs."

"I didn't make plans to do a candle party on Sunday!"

"Don't disappoint me, Nikki. I was there for you when you needed me, be a friend, see ya."

That little shyster, typical Craig! He jogged away fast before I could really say what I wanted to him. He did it again!
What a jerk.
I went back into the house. Ten minutes later, the UPS truck came by my place with a package. "Just sign here, ma'am." He said, handing me the electronic tablet. "Thank you."

He handed me the yellow padded envelope, which was postmarked from Santa Barbara and had the address of the hotel where Paul had been for his two-week training seminar. Inside the envelope was a little white box with a neatly wrapped sheer golden ribbon around it. I opened the box, and under the delicate gold tissue paper was a beautiful light pink sea glass necklace. It was beautiful. Hanging from a delicate silver chain, the piece of sea glass
had a silver wire-like design wrapped around it. The glass was very unique, it was shaped like a heart and had a small pink diamond in the middle of it. Also inside the padded envelope was a note that read:

I went surfing early in the morning, I caught
A few really cool waves, and on my way in, I found this piece of pink

*sea glass down at my feet. Half of it was in the sand, and the other half
was barely visible. I was surprised to see it in the shape of a heart. It
seemed special or unique; either way, it reminded me of you. So I took
it to a jeweler and had them make a necklace in silver, and the pink
diamond, well, that was a little something extra for being such a big
help on this case we were on. Plus, I never did get a chance to take you
on that fancy dinner in Laguna. I remember how much you loved the
glass we collected at the beach that day we went surfing, so I hope you
like it.*

See you soon, babe. Thanks again

Paul

I picked up my phone and sent him a text message...

LOVE THE NECKLACE, I'LL THINK OF YOU

EVERY TIME I WEAR IT. Nikki...

P.S. How about a rain check on that dinner in Laguna?

I wore a white halter-style dress and a black wrap from
Nordstrom that I got yesterday for a mere $25, don't you just love
clearances? Yeah, right, I also had a $100.00 gift card from
Martin and Oliver from last Christmas to cover the rest of the cost. I
added a pair of black sandals and headed out.
I drove with the top down on the bug (my favorite way to travel, of
course). On to Matt's housewarming party. The neighborhood was

pretty nice, and parking was ample, something my condo didn't have. Maybe it was time to purchase a house, I thought.

"You look beautiful," Matt said, opening the front door for me to his new, fully decorated home.

"Thank you."

Music was blaring to the sounds of the latest dance music, and then changed to an old Beach Boys tune of "Wouldn't it be Nice". Walking through the new house, Matt was telling me of all the new changes and the furniture, which was more contemporary but with a few Spanish-style touches.

The living room had a large L-shaped couch in grey with two navy blue decorative pillows. The coffee table was dark wood, and the walls had pictures of us and pictures of friends he had at the department. The open floor plan flowed nicely, the kitchen had stainless steel appliances and dark wood cabinets with light countertops in quartz, with plenty of sunlight coming from the double French doors out to the patio. Instead of a dining table, there was a large green-top pool table already filled with people playing doubles.

The party was in full swing, most of the guests I knew, and just a few I didn't. I walked out to the patio, where the smell of steaks and grilled chicken was cooking to perfection. A large table had bowls of chips, dips, and a large fruit platter. Smaller patio tables had guests seated, with their drinks, and the pool had a game of Marco Polo in progress.

"Let's get you a drink." Matt said,

"Ok, just a ..."

"Coke." He finished.

Handing me one from the small fridge in the outdoor kitchen. "Thank You." I cracked it open and refueled. Party tunes blared from inside the house out to the outdoor speakers that were above the patio.

"You did a nice job here on the sound system."

"Thanks, I had professionals come in to do it."

We sat on barstools at the outdoor kitchen bar that was topped with drink mixes, a silver blender, and glasses.

"The house looks great, Matt. I love the outdoor kitchen and the pool; it's so California. A tall brunette walked by me and then stopped. She turned to me and asked. "Excuse me, is that a sea glass heart?"

"Yes, it is," I said, looking down at my necklace from Paul that I wore tonight. The music changed to bro-country, Thomas Rhett, Crash and Burn, and I swear if fate doesn't make the right song come on as a precursor to men's moods.

"Oh my gosh, hey Maria, you have to see this," she said, calling out to her friend by the grill.

She came over to admire my necklace. Matt just stood by my side quietly.

"That's beautiful, I love the pink diamond in the middle of the heart.

I've seen lots of sea glass necklaces, but none with diamonds; that's really cool. I guess whoever gave that to you must love you. Pink diamonds are worth a lot, too,"

Maria and her friend said.

After complimenting my jewelry, they fled to get a drink.

I spotted Jessica, and she came over to Matt and me.

"Hi Matt, hi Nikki, I haven't had a chance to catch up with you, girl, we have to talk."

"I know it's been pretty crazy," I told her, drinking my Coke.

"That is a pretty necklace, Nikki." Jessica spotted it right away. "Thank you." I hesitated to tell her who it was from.
"Is that from you, Matt?" Jessica asked.
Matt responded

"No, it's not my gift."
Jessica got the message right away and changed the subject,
"So how are you doing? I haven't seen you since last week."

"I've been lying low."
Matt looked a bit annoyed and moved along to the grill to check on his steaks. And yet another song came on, you know what happened. Oh yeah, the jukebox was full of laughs today, as Eye of the Tiger from the movie Rocky III came on.
"Wow, so you got that from Det. Anderson."

"Yes, I think Matt is jealous I've been getting compliments left and right. He looks mad, what do you think?"

"Yikes, looks like you're in a lover's triangle."

"No more like the Bermuda Triangle." We both chuckled.

"So what are you going to do?'

"I don't know, Matt and I broke up, and then I met Paul, and then now all of a sudden Matt wants me back. It's crazy, I think I'm going to just keep both at a distance until I know what it is I really want, I mean, right?"

"Yeah, just remember you're in control, uh oh he's looking this way, oh he's coming over."

We both put on cheesy smiles and pretended to be talking about the new accessories store in the mall.

"Ok, ladies' dinner is now ready, go ahead and grab a plate, I have potato salad, fresh fruit, and lots of good stuff,"

"Thank you, Matt," I said, feeling good.

Jessica got up and went to the table filled with salads and plates, forks, etc. I saw Roxy and her new date coming out of the French doors. Arriving late as usual.

And we were back to rockin' country, on XM, I'm getting my ex back radio. Matt came close to me; he's much taller than me, 6'2 to be exact, so he whispered in my ear.

"Can you give Anderson a message for me?" Matt asked.

He wasn't smiling or joking; his face was serious with intent and bordered on massive testosterone like a bloating peacock.

I was a little curious why all this secretive whispering, but I said, "Sure, what is it, Matt?"

"Tell him it's ON."

I turned to look at him, confused. It's on. What did he mean by that?

"What does that mean?" I asked with a confused look on my face

"It means I want my girl back." He winked.

He took a swig of his beer and went to join his guests in the pool.

I stood there still and was surprised by his words. Now I had a problem, and the pressure of it was going to build.

He would be pushing, and now I would have to come to terms with choosing.

I shivered at the passing breeze and a dark, passing cloud that flowed above us, making its way to the foothill mountains.

I knew a scary storm was a comin'......

EPILOGUE

I opened the morning paper to find quite a story and a bit of irony. On the front page of the Rancho Niguel Courier read:

Tragedy in the Mayor's office once again!

Last night was yet another unfortunate turn of events for the Mayor of Rancho Niguel. At 8:15 pm, Mayor Grant Mahoney and his wife, Veronica Mahoney, were on their way to Palm Springs for a start to the campaign trail for the great Governor's race.

Traveling on Highway 10 East in the third lane, a drunk driver veered off and sideswiped the Mahoney's Black Cadillac. The Mahoneys' driver swerved and tried to gain control of the vehicle, but then hit the center divider, where it came to a stop. Mayor Mahoney and the driver had minor injuries, but the Mayor's wife sustained serious injury and was pronounced dead on the way to the Hospital. We are all very saddened by this, and we send our thoughts and prayers to the Mahoney family at this time. The other driver was intoxicated and had minor injuries he was treated for. There is no word yet on funeral arrangements for Mrs. Mahoney, but we will bring them to you as soon as they are available.

Mayor Mahoney has dropped out of the Governor's race and would like privacy at this time of mourning.

Wow! I couldn't believe what I read, how strange he was going to leave his wife to be free of her, and yet fate had this all along. My cell rang, it was Roxy.

"Hey, girl, have you read the paper this morning?"

"Oh my God, yes! Can you believe this?'

"I know it's so sad and strange."

"My words exactly!

On A much lighter note, I got a call from the city for the retirement party, and we have the gig, and we get to dress in

Halloween costumes, how fun is that?"

"Oh, I can't wait, but what are we going as?"

"How about something scary!"

Don't miss the next exciting

Nikki Rodriguez Mystery,

Teammates, Terror, and Thriller

It was a long, hot summer, but now the leaves have turned brown, the temperature has cooled, and Fall is bringing more than just Pumpkin Spice Lattes. It's October, and Halloween is just around the corner in Rancho Niguel. Singer Nikki Rodriguez is in for more trouble when she finds the body of her old college swim teammate floating in a pool on a stormy day. Determined to find the one responsible, Nikki is once again searching for clues and following leads. Along with the help of her old friends and her new boyfriend, Detective Paul Anderson. Everyone in Rancho Niguel is ready for ghouls, witches, goblins, and vampires. Halloween is filled with tricks and treats, and Nikki finds more than she bargained for. With the Halloween Harvest Festival and the Witches Brew Ball retirement party for Tank and Brinks, and who can forget Captain Matt Stevens, who is still declaring his love for her, Nikki has her plate full. Yet all is not what it seems, and soon secrets will be uncovered, and hearts will be broken. One thing is true: there's nothing scarier than trying to catch a killer.